D0045000

BANKROLL

ALSO BY BRUCE DUCKER

Rule by Proxy
Failure at the Mission Trust

BANKROLL

Bruce Ducker

E. P. DUTTON   NEW YORK

Published in the United States by E. P. Dutton,
a division of Penguin Books USA Inc.,
2 Park Avenue, New York, N.Y. 10016.

Published simultaneously in Canada by
Fitzhenry and Whiteside, Limited, Toronto.

Library of Congress Cataloging-in-Publication Data
Ducker, Bruce.
Bankroll / Bruce Ducker. — 1st ed.
p.   cm.
ISBN 0-525-24789-0
I. Title.
PS3554.U267B36   1989
813'.54—dc19   89-1215
CIP

1 3 5 7 9 10 8 6 4 2

First Edition

Lyrics from "God Bless the Child" by Billie Holiday and Arthur Herzog, Jr.,
used by permission. Copyright 1941 by Edward B. Marks Music Company,
copyright renewed. All rights reserved.

New York

1

"You know what your trouble is?" Shelley asked.

Spector knew. At least he could make a hell of a guess. Indecision, flagging ambition, ennui. An undercut backhand that set up high . . .

"You've had it too easy."

"Oh, no, Shelley. Not the Great Depression speech."

Spector faced the deli's plate-glass window. A short Hispanic man was mopping the outside of the glass with a rubber squeegee, and soapsuds ran across the walk into the street.

"Too easy."

"You're probably right," Spector said without conviction.

"I know I'm right. I know I'm right. Start off with summa cum laude . . ."

"Magna."

"Magna." Shelley shrugged him off. It didn't signify.

The waiter placed their sandwiches in front of them, checked his pad, walked on. Spector looked at the two wedges on Shelley's plate. Corned beef on rye bread. Two open mouths, yawning at him.

"You marry a beautiful, intelligent woman. Her father's brains, I'll give you that, but brains. You get a job with the Street's hottest firm."

All true. Shelley dropped his jaw to its limits and fit his teeth

3

around the sandwich. The brief silence gave Spector a chance to rebut, but he had nothing to say. Shelley could chew and talk at the same time, like the ventriloquist who sips water while his puppet hums.

"And you're good at it. Smart-ass right out of some fancy school, and he's good at it. Now all he has to do is hang around, he makes a cool zillion, he's set."

"Shelley, you're right."

"I know I'm right. You know I'm right. How many kids your age—How old are you?"

"Thirty-one."

"Thirty-one. How many thirty-one-year-olds own a Murray Hill co-op, views, three bedrooms, six seventy-five?"

"I don't."

"You don't because you gave it away. That's another thing. You give it up. It's one thing to be a Gentile. It's another to make it your profession."

Spector laughed. The window cleaner finished, tossed a rag into his pail, walked off. A man on the sidewalk carrying a Bible was shouting at the passersby. The few who regarded him did so with contempt. It put Spector in mind of a television camera some talk show had pointed at the street. Everyone was on the air on his way to work. Except you couldn't change the channel. Shelley went on.

"Look, I understand people get divorced, people don't get along. Joanie was the baby, we didn't do her any favors giving her what we did. She's not easy to live with, and I don't mean to speak against my own daughter. But you."

Here he swallowed in exasperation.

"You. You walk away. You give everything to her. Does that make sense?"

Their waiter came by. Shelley stopped him with a look.

"You not gonna ask us how's everything?"

"You need, you'll ask."

Spector spoke up. "I ordered a cream soda."

"Waiter, get this man a cream soda."

"Shelley, I told him."

The waiter didn't move. He eyed their plates.

"You don't like the turkey club?"

"The turkey club is fine," Spector said. "We've been talking. Just a cream soda."

The waiter pursed his lips, considering the request. Why wasn't the man eating? Spector picked up the sandwich in two hands and took a bite. The waiter nodded and left.

"The paintings, the Tabriz rugs, all the wedding gifts."

"I didn't need a Cuisinart, Shelley."

"Too easy. Why do you walk out of a job like that?"

"I was bored."

"He was bored. He makes more money than the Federal Reserve, and he was bored. Do you know how much I was netting out of brass fittings when I had been at it four years? How long had you been at it?"

"Four years?"

"Do you know how much?"

Again he smiled. There was nothing else to do. He knew what was coming.

"And the marriage? That bored you too?"

"Your daughter wanted the divorce." They both knew better. Joan had first conceived of the divorce, but as a throwaway, a bright idea. Once the thought was on the table, Spector became its advocate. He liked solutions. Maybe if he had said no, it wouldn't have happened.

"And you went along with it?" Shelley asked.

"We don't chain wives to the radiator any more. I know it was done when you were a youth in Rumania."

"Bensonhurst."

"Bensonhurst. But today it's regarded as *de trop*."

By the entrance stood a couple, impatient for a table. They both caught Spector's eye. They tried to stare him into repentance or, better, speed. He looked away, took a second bite of the turkey club.

"I'll tell you something. If you'd had a few failures along the way, you wouldn't spit in the eye of success. You'd be more respectful."

Spector leaned forward and motioned him closer, as if to tell a secret. He put his hand on the back of the older man's hand and patted it. His friend leaned too.

"You're a wonderful man," Spector said. "As a father-in-law I liked you. As a non-father-in-law I like you even better. But as a philosopher you're all field, no hit."

Shelley smiled at him. Bright-red specks of corned beef showed through his irregular teeth.

"So, if I'm such a lightweight, what do you want my advice on?"

"Who wants your advice? I'll get a free lunch, a reminder of how I'm squandering the best years of my life, and chronic indigestion for a week."

The older man nodded and waited.

"I merely thought I'd ask your views on what I ought to do."

"My views."

"This would go faster if you didn't repeat everything I said."

"First you want my views, then you tell me how to give them. Well, let's see. What can we eliminate? Investment banking—there you work with your head, and it's boring. What else can we scratch? Anything you can make some dough at. Joanie claims you were a hell of a tennis player."

Spector dismissed the idea, shaking his head. "Small-town stuff."

"Scratch Wimbledon. I got it. Why don't you come into brass fittings? We don't use brains. We just shout. And business is always lousy. You won't make a dime. It sounds made to order."

"It's a good thing I'm not paying for this lunch."

"You've made that clear. Let's take a closer look. What kind of businesses do you know about?"

"Are you serious? I've been doing M-and-A work. Mergers and acquisitions. I don't know about any business."

The older man was quiet while he finished the last bites of the sandwich. He put the crust back on the plate, nestled with its twin, and held his fist to his chest.

"So what have you merged?"

"Financial-service companies, mostly."

"Financial-service."

"Investment advisers, software suppliers, thrifts. Banks."

"Banks."

"Banks. Look, Shelley, there's nothing more boring than working for a bank."

"Who said 'working.' Did I say 'working'? You want some pie?" Spector shook his head. "The pie isn't bad. It's not the pickles, but it's not bad. You know what Willie Sutton said when they asked him why he robbed banks?"

"Because that's where the money is," Spector answered.

"You got it."

6

"You think I should rob banks?"

"Better than working."

"You've been a great help."

"Me and Doctor Ruth."

The waiter came, tore a slip off his pad, and put it by Shelley's elbow. Shelley ignored the bill, leaving it face down. From his hip wallet he took out two tens and placed them on the table like the winning pair.

"Look. I meant that about our business."

"Meant what?"

"You want to come in with us, I'd love to have you. A *shaigitz* like you would ruin the business in a month, but you'd give us some class. We don't have any tennis players."

"Thank you. I appreciate that."

They walked out together into the summer street. The heat rose from the sidewalk, from the sides of cars, from the bodies of the jostling people. At the corner a vendor was roasting giant pretzels. Crusted salt glistened like diamond dust.

"Not that you'd want it. It's a tough business."

"I don't think it's for me."

Shelley shrugged. "Who's it for? You look like Montgomery Clift, you went to some college that resembles Central Park, it's got no subways, and you got Latin words on your diploma. Go rob banks. It's not for me either."

"I'm grateful. Every so often a man can use an offer he can turn down. Helps the ego."

He shook the older man's hand. Shelley had begun to sweat through at the armpits of his no-iron shirt.

"You need any money?"

"No thanks."

"You got some? You didn't let Joanie take it all? I'm surprised you haven't given it away. That's a good sign."

"I've got some."

"Okay. Look, keep in touch. Let me know."

"I will."

2

What was it Fitzgerald said about New York on a summer weekend? Overripe, like waiting for something to fall into your hands.

Spector walked back from the Central Park courts carrying only a racquet and a towel. This was a part of his slow withdrawal from life as a clubman. Little by little. He kept his membership, but his tennis was now played on the hard and sooty courts afforded him by the Parks Department. Too, he had a seven-block walk to his apartment to shower, and nowhere to put his valuables. Come to think of it, though, he hadn't any valuables. Then the challenge was to avoid the bores who inhabited the men's lounge. Now it was the kids who whizzed by him on skateboards, cautioning him, in not unfriendly tones, Watch it, motherfucker. Which was the greater hazard? Is there any risk greater than boredom?

One thing was certain. Competition on the public courts ended with the match. He had struck up a weekly game with a man named Lauren, a black man with a ferocious first serve and a second that angled off like a flying buttress. They didn't discuss the markets, their histories, or their vocations. They played tennis. If they talked afterwards, it was at random and easily. And it was about the strategy, the score, and their next-Saturday's rendezvous. None of the collegial chatter of the club rooms, with its encrypted interrogation to find out who had had the more profitable week, who could glean a piece of news from whom.

8

There was also the fact that his new opponent was someone he never would have faced across the nets at the Racquet Club. That was a bonus.

At Eighty-sixth street, he jogged west to Broadway to the market. He would eat breakfast in, read the paper, and think about his future. Shelley's advice had not moved him forward an inch, and while he felt no pressing need to go to work, each day spent exercising, serving a bucket of balls, doing the *Times* crossword led with increasing momentum to another, identical day.

The brown bag swayed with the discreet weight of breakfast for one. A small casaba melon, a cup of vanilla yogurt, a freshly baked bran muffin, and two large containers of coffee. He picked up his paper in the foyer, this Saturday beating out the late-sleeping competition, and bounded up the two flights. Where was all this energy in the third set?

Inside his apartment, Spector set the Formica table with precision. He placed one coffee container in the microwave and hit two minutes. He would save the second for later. He set out a carving knife for the melon and a spoon. On a single plate he put the muffin and the cardboard yogurt-cup, and spread his paper out so that its pages didn't interfere with the table service. The melon halved with a satisfying thunk.

The lead column carried a story on the Persian Gulf. He skipped it. Maybe he'd come back later, but Iran was not relevant to his personal situation and not germane to profit-taking. That, for several years, was the way he had taken on the news. The lesson of his time on Wall Street was that every political, natural, or economic dislocation brought opportunity. The smart money figured out what reaction was needed. Profit opportunities could spawn in a typhoon through Burma's rice belt, in New York City's debt crisis, in the decision of a sociopathic brain to plant cyanide in a packaged medicine. Good times and bad, Black Monday, Maundy Thursday. One merely had to be smart, cynical, quick, and rich.

Spector figured he was three out of four.

The second lead was a story he'd been following. Several insiders had struck a deal on a plea. He knew one. Not well, but well enough. Thirty-six years old, the man was going up for abuse of insider information. He had pocketed almost nine mil-

9

lion from buying calls on a stock that turned up as a target in a takeover. Abuse of insider information. He could hear Shelley's voice: Who wants outsider information?

Was it worth it? Why would someone who had made seven figures a year legally for most of his professional career and could continue to do so—why would he risk it all? Spector knew. Absolutely. The rush. Going over the top of the hill in the front seat of the roller coaster.

When you did your first deal it was there. By your tenth it was still around but only at closing. When the check passed, when the board changed hands. By your thirtieth the Lucite tombstone got stored in your drawer, the Taittinger tasted sharp. This guy didn't need the nine million. He needed the high. And now he's off to Danbury.

What is the lesson here, children? Easy: don't get caught.

Is that all we can learn from today's reading? Isn't there a second message, subtle but there? This guy thought the caper, done right, was worth the risk.

The microwave beeped. He took out the coffee and poured it into a mug. He pulled out one of the four matching chairs, done in a red plastic he thought they reserved for diner booths, sat down, and thumbed idly through the rest of the paper. When he reached the book page, he took the MontBlanc pen from the breast pocket of his bathrobe. She hadn't left with everything of value, he thought.

In five minutes he had eaten the slice of melon, half the yogurt, and the entire muffin. And he had inked in the cross-word. He turned back to the front-page news. Was there anything he'd missed? Maybe Shelley was right. But he couldn't see himself in handcuffs, clasping a raincoat over his head to hide his face, rushing up the steps at Foley Square.

He put a plastic wrap over the uneaten melon half and placed it and the yogurt in the refrigerator. They stood next to two bottles of club soda and one of tonic. A regular pantry. He ran hot water over the plate, coursing away the melon seeds, and left it and the mug in the sink. One plate and one glass per meal, two meals per day. Dinner out—he couldn't stand his apartment at night. You ran the dishwasher maybe once a week. Count the passing of time by the sound of the dishwasher. The priests of Chichén Itzá gave out gourds to their followers. Every sunrise, smash a gourd. When you have no more, plant your fields.

The calendar of the modern man. After seven days, run the dishwasher. After seven runnings, go to the market for frozen foods. After seven visits, celebrate the new year.

Funny. It was just that rut that had led Joan to suggest calling it quits and him to agree. They didn't divorce as much as they gave up.

When the Babylonian astronomers realized their calendar was slipping behind, they simply decreed an extra month. An intercalary. Maybe that's what he needed. An intercalary life.

She didn't understand him either.

"You walk out of your firm and leave all those dollars for your partners. Now you're going to walk away from a marriage as if it were a book you didn't want to finish."

It was true. Leave it to Joan to put it in proper syntax. And when he left Joan he had intended to leave behind everything of value. All with her. The Bertoia chairs, the Ben Shahn lithographs, the carved jade collection that he didn't like in the Queen Anne highboy that he did, the compact-disc player, and the entire collection of Beethoven sonatas that went with it. He used to love the sonatas, but lately he envied their passion and was happy to put them behind him. Everything, except his jazz records and the pen. The records she delivered. He had walked out that last night with the pen in his coat.

In his last months at the firm nothing stirred his blood. At first he had thought it the perfect job. The stakes were large, the people intense. There were winners and losers. On one of his deals, where his firm engineered the takeover of a chain of New Jersey thrifts for a major money-center bank, he had met Joan. A Wharton M.B.A. with the scent of Je Reviens. Hired to do strategic planning, she had devised a plan that showed the owners the profit they could make by finding a large bank to buy them out. Spector was working Stanley while she worked Livingstone. It was the perfect match. And that, of course, was what he had grown used to and, in the last, tired of: perfection.

Their relationship followed the same index of excitement as the merger. It made a lot of sense on paper. And it was exciting at first. As it turned out, the wedding was the closing.

11

The marriage was merely the living out of someone else's projections.

Now, after the counseling, months after the split, long after he had resigned from the firm, what was he doing? Microwaving meals. Rereading newspapers. And attacking the *Times* crossword. Five minutes for the daily. Maybe half an hour for Sunday's.

Come on, man. Action is the antidote for self-pity. He fell to the woven mat on his living room floor and, face set, did twenty-five push-ups and twenty-five sit-ups. Just do that every day, add maybe five sets of each a week. Before you know it, fifty sit-ups, fifty push-ups.

He took a leisurely shower, then lay down on his bed. The air conditioner gasped. It was only eleven o'clock, Saturday morning. The city was empty. Maybe he should have accepted one of those invitations. Bridgehampton, the Vineyard, Bayhead. He picked up a *New York* magazine and turned to the last page for the puzzle. Instead, with an uncharacteristic curiosity about how others lead their lives, he began to browse the classified advertisements.

And three lines there gave him an idea.

Where it had come from, Spector couldn't say. That passing remark of Shelley's, perhaps. In Spector's life, the shadow between thought and reality had been the merest pause. What he considered doing, he did. Was that, he wondered, why the pause between the peak and the descent was similarly brief?

The idea was remarkable not for the profit it bespoke. Those thoughts had been his inventory, his profession, for several years. The idea instead demanded the same analysis, the same knowledge of an industry, the very ability to run, at high speed, various scenarios and to assure one had planned for the likely contingencies. But this idea was different. It was, in the peremptory language of the law, a felony. Maybe it would be more fun.

The advertisement preceded the hundreds of personals. That feral section disturbed him, its sophisticated young males with languid afternoons, its handsome Christian widows of artistic preferences seeking widowers with same. This ad was in the Services Wanted section, a short, bloodless listing of people seeking nannies, dogwalkers, car parkers. Nestled at the end was the germ of an idea.

WANTED: rspnsble cpl for house-sitting in
exchng for rent. Sml Wst Sd Apt. Refs
Reqd. Box 131-m.

Not the plan. Just the germ. There were several problems
with this request. First, they were looking for a couple. He no
longer qualified. Second, references. He needed someone he
could overwhelm with credentials. The third weakness—the un-
forgivable weakness—was economic. A West Side residence did
not suit the bill. And people who were so cheap that they ab-
breviated everything where the full treatment would have cost
thirty bucks were not his people. This wasn't quite it.

But it was a place to begin. In an hour he was at the peri-
odicals desk of the Forty-second Street library. The search wasn't
as easy as he had imagined. The logical way to do this was a
readership profile, but he thought he knew enough about up-
scale magazines to get started. *Connoisseur*, *Vogue*, and *Vanity Fair*,
he was disappointed to find, carried no personals. Back issues
of *New York* magazine had a limited selection. *Texas Monthly* and
National Review proved the idea could work, but one was too
distant and the other too cautious. The *Saturday Review* was a
bonanza. Overcoming a strong urge to attack the unmarked
Double-Crostics, he made a note of descriptions and box numbers.

He stopped off on the way back to his apartment to open
a post office box. He knew he would need an identity for this
first phase. He determined not to pick an arbitrary name and
seized instead on that of a fellow alumnus of his college, one
whose letter soliciting contributions for dear old alma mater had
been in his mailbox that very morning.

He knew nothing of Roger Weedman except what was in
that letter. Roger was earnest, a great supporter of the school,
a member of the Class of 1974 (six years his senior), and, from
the letterhead, a young and doubtless rising partner at one of
the largest law firms in Houston. Who better?

By four o'clock a slight breeze had cooled that muggy afternoon, and, unbeknownst to Roger Weedman, Roger Weedman
had rented a mailbox at the Grand Central Station post office.
He had filled in and mailed half a dozen credit-card applications.
And he had sent out four inquiries, each identical except as to
address and geographic detail.

Dear sir,

I write in response to your advertisement in the *Saturday Review*.

I am an author by trade and am prepared to take up residence in your house during your absence in order to be able to conclude work on a project now under way. No compensation would be necessary. I can do light maintenance chores and assure that mail delivery, house plants, etc., go attended.

I am particularly eager to work in Scarsdale/Cape Ann/Lake Forest/upstate New York, because of the proximity it affords to New York's libraries/the sea/Northwestern University/the solitude of the countryside. I feel those surroundings would be conducive to finishing this work within the allotted time. With, of course, your permission, I would like to list your hospitality in the acknowledgments in my book when published.

My work is concerned with medieval Frankish history, and in particular the period of Charlemagne. My second book was nominated for the Samuel Eliot Morison Prize for History. I am a graduate of Swarthmore College, and you should feel free to corroborate this fact and any others with the Alumni Office of the College, 215-555-1480.

Yours faithfully,
Roger M. Weedman

3

He awoke sensing the keen edge of a new love affair. Or so he recalled—it had been a long time. The sun's morning rays bounced off windows across the street to stir him, and he was cured of the malady that had seen that light as drab. His plan was the antidote to aid his recovery, and contemplation of the illicit was a tonic.

He drafted lists of things to do and posted them on his refrigerator, and the days ended before he could complete the tasks he had set down. He purchased a box of computer form paper, and by tearing and taping soon had lengthy charts lining the whitewashed walls of his apartment. Time charts, perk charts, probability studies. The living room, without a picture since he had moved in, and with the spare furniture—two dissimilar coffee tables and a chifforobe—that was, the landlady had said proudly, only fifty dollars more, began to look like the war room of his old firm.

He pasted his outline left to right across the wall, so he could see its chronology. Each phase was also divided horizontally, by heavy red lines, into three sections. At the top he listed the tasks, in the middle the related budget, and at the bottom the risks. His first chart looked like this:

WEEDMAN APPEARS

1. Make contact—how many mailings? Three wks per.
2. References—need?
3. Medieval history—different field next time?
4. Interviews.

BUDGET

Research	$ 250
Stationery	500
Printing	500
Travel (4 trips max., per miling)	4000
TOTAL	$5250

RISKS

1. Story doesn't hold up
    Weedman checked
    References checked
    Preparation inadequate
2. Bond or other identification required?
3. What's the penalty? Do I care?

He thought about a section for timing, but in fact the pace of the plan was beyond his control. Most likely none of the four he had written would respond to his inquiry, so he would have to do additional mailings. If that turned out to be true, he had time galore. Time to research the right bank, time to construct the necessary mechanism to handle the funds, even time to learn something about Charlemagne. What had moved him to choose that odd subject as his specialty?

The longer he had to search for his host, the more it would cost, and the greater the risk of exposure. The dangers did not unduly upset him. He enjoyed estimating risk and living with his estimates. For a few years he had made his living that way, and he didn't understand those who found decisions difficult. Each one led down a new path, and it was the path, not the destination, that had always caught his interest.

For the expense he had no concern. There was money in the bank, and it was to spend. Nothing, of course, like what he had earned. Although he had been one of the industry's fastest young gunsels, he had remarkably little to show for it. Where the hell had it gone? The house in Sag Harbor they had used three times. Only once together. The parties with that string quartet that insisted on playing the School of Paris composers. Joan was easily led. He too.

It was difficult to say. At the end there weren't many hard assets. Some decent paintings. A significant margin account with the arbitrageurs. A second with his firm's commodities section. That one had netted him enormous stacks of trading records, a lot of action until the market broke, and a short-term loss carry-forward that would see most players through the Second Coming.

The money had flowed in fast. Earning it was easy. Not enjoyable, easy. They had spent it the same way.

Joan had resented that he was not more reverent. She sorted their earnings into accounts and tallied up complicated long and short positions. He had thought her prudent at first, then deferential. In the end, her odd, commercial piety had been one of the few things he had criticized. And in the end, when she had divided their funds into substatements, their bankbooks into stacks, it was only her diligence that had resulted in the twenty thousand in his account.

No, small change wasn't a problem. Thanks, Joan, for the little things.

More promptly than he could have hoped, there was a response in his mailbox. The Scarsdale couple. They asked for references and enclosed a bonding form for Weedman to complete. A cautious pair. Scratched.

Spector could have gotten the books he needed from the library, but for all he knew the New York Public kept computer records forever. Safer to leg it over to Barnes and Noble and buy the books. For cash—no records. He took what was in stock: Katherine Pyle's biography of Charlemagne, *The Commercial Loan Officer's Handbook*, and a textbook on lending policies put out by the American Bankers' Association.

Spector threw himself into the research as if it were a new acquisition problem. He pored through texts, taking notes and making outlines. The activity gave him the comfort of the familiar and a sense of motion. He had treated mergers the same way. Gather material. Read their sales manuals, SEC filings, interim financial statements. You might never use what you learn. But you might, and it quieted the anxiety about the larger issues. Only when you were ready for the exam, for what they might ask, were you ready to meet the opposition.

He grew hungry four or five times a day. And each time he was surprised to find there was nothing to eat in his apartment. Down to the street: a candy bar, a frozen lasagna, a sixpack of Popsicles.

The project began to take form. He walked through the possibilities, thinking of additional risks while sleeping, awakening himself, and writing down thoughts on a pad he kept by the bed. He had written a dream diary one year in college, and the discipline of recall and recapture served him well. Now he reviewed each risk until, like a bespoke tailor, he had measured it and knew its dimensions.

Spector estimated the days needed for a response, and determined to make a second mailing to prospects three weeks after the first letters would have missed their mark. With that would come a new cycle of advertisers in the personals. In numbers there was success. If there are twenty horses in a race, and you tell each of twenty people that a different horse will win, one soul will think you a visionary.

How many mailings would he need before he found the right home?

Two days after Scarsdale, bright and early, he was at Weedman's post office. There was a second letter in the box. It was written in a man's plain hand and, in an atavistic and companionable touch, with a fountain pen.

Dear Roger Weedman,
     Thank you for your letter of last Thursday. We would be very interested in the possibility of your caring for our house while we are on our cruise. Do you like cats?
     There isn't much to do, and the neighbors would help you out if you got in a jam. I'll be in New York on the 4th of next month and I could meet with you then. Write and give me your telephone number so I can call and we can meet. Swarthmore says hello.
                                        Sincerely,
                                        Edgar M. Parish

The return address was embossed: 129 Parmalee Road, Lake Forest, Ill. 60045. So was, discreetly under the envelope flap, the name of the New York jeweler who had manufactured the stationery. This may not be the one, Spector thought, but it ain't a bad start.

Hello, Mr. Parish. I think you'd better sit down.

Spector intended to construct a more elaborate *nom de guerre*, and had set about the details with a dramatist's flair. He had priced the possibility of having false reviews of Weedman-authored books set in print. He was particularly keen on having one with his photograph, not the least because he envied the persona he had created for Roger Weedman. But as he looked at the calendar, he realized that he would have to try himself out on Parish without props. If he missed, if the Parish letter came to naught, he could better prepare for the next target. The New York visit was only six days away.

He couldn't send Parish an address or a telephone number without leaving traces. That left two alternatives. Get on a plane and visit him in Lake Forest, making some excuse about why he happened to be in the neighborhood, or call him and arrange for a New York meeting. The first would be too aggressive. He had, after all, proposed to move into the man's house. To appear uninvited at his door might diminish his character and emphasize his appetite.

But Parish had supplied no telephone number. A quick check with Illinois Bell confirmed that he was unlisted.

All this Spector considered in the blocks from the post office to his apartment. He was concentrating on these variations in his plans, and so was unmindful of the kids throwing a tennis ball against the stoop. One of the kids, a fielder, backed up for a pop fly and bumped him. Spector reached up and one-handed the ball. They had rules for an interfering car—the play went over—but none for an interfering pedestrian. Curses followed him up the stairwell.

He was too excited to wait. He retrieved the Hartman attaché case from under the bed. Joan had sent his matching luggage by cab. One thing you had to say about her. Everything in its place. From a wall he tore that page of the chart that described the Roger Weedman he had created, and packed it along with some sharpened pencils and notepaper. He ran from the apartment through the resumed game. Outside, the day had cooked up to its summer heat, like a Crockpot stew. Damn, he thought. He had none of his tropical worsteds back from storage. Joan used to take care of that.

The cab dropped him at the library, and he bounded up the steps into the Beaux-Arts entrance at Forty-first Street. Where would he be without his research skills and this grand facility? So the people shall know. Someday he would have to thank the library's benefactors. He knew one or two from charity events, another pastime he and Joan had found to put otherwise neutral activities between them.

The reference room contained city directories and telephone books for every major U.S. community. The Yellow Pages for the Chicago area listed three full columns of "Clubs—Private." It was a long shot. He copied down the names and numbers of twenty-six; the rest excluded themselves. Professional Women's Club. Serbo-Croatian Recreation Club. University of Chicago Faculty Club.

Back to the apartment. Three o'clock, two o'clock Chicago time. Exactly right. No one in the bars but the help. He began calling.

"Is Mr. Parish there?"

"Is he a member, sir? I don't know him."

"I believe he is. Edgar Parish."

"No one is here now, sir."

"Give me his home number, will you?"

"I'm sorry, sir. We have no Edgar Parish in the roster."

"Sorry to bother you."

He called through the list with the phone pinned to his shoulder. His neck began to cramp midway, and he switched ears. There were three places left. No response at the obvious ones, the Lake Forest Country Club, the larger town clubs. He was down to the Union Hill.

"Is Mr. Edgar Parish there?"

"Senior or junior?"

"Senior." The writing on the letter before him was unsteady, erratically spaced.

"No, sir. May I say who is calling?"

"Yes. I'm calling from New York. Give me his home number, will you?"

"I'm sorry, sir. We don't give out that information."

"Don't be silly. Who is this?"

"Jerry, sir."

"Oh, yes, Jerry. Now, Jerry. This is Mr. Wrigley. Give me his home number on Parmalee Drive."

"Excuse me, sir. Of course. Just a minute. Here it is." The seven digits followed.

Spector sat back in the wing chair. Exhausted, exhilarated. He hadn't had so much fun, or been on such an edge, since his first contested tender offer. His team had won.

On the spur of the moment he had had to come up with a name known to any Chicago club barman. There were enough of them in the public domain—Otis, Swift, Pullman. He'd been able to think of only one. Thank heaven for a little baseball trivia.

4

Spector was five minutes early for the match. Still, as always, Lauren was there first, stretching out. Court time was at a premium, and you were advised to be prompt or lose your place. They shook hands and exchanged a brief greeting. Spector kneeled into a hurdler's stretch by his friend.

"Ideal temperature."

"Be hot by nine."

"Lucky to get this time."

Lauren returned his conspiratorial smile. In the world of public courts, he had said, recognizing the naïveté of his pupil in these matters, a little baksheesh goes a long way. And so after each session they tipped the Parks man ten bucks, and by their charity had held on to two hours every Saturday morning at eight. Spector protested that it wasn't right, and Lauren charged him with prep-school ethics.

"You get your choice. You can keep your principles or the court. Not both."

Since the start of their weekly matches, intense and silent, Spector had had the edge. He had played competitive tennis from the time he turned twelve, and he knew how to turn the opponent's energies against him. He lured Lauren into mistakes, and so long as his adversary obliged, Spector had the advantage.

He judged Lauren to be about his age, newer to the game but the better athlete. Spector led on form, on Aristotelian analysis, on strokes. But the lanky man, now hitting forehands across the net to him, had an ability which he sensed would eventually overpower him. Even now the shots came longer, the weight hitting on his racquet like a croquet ball, wooden, antagonistic. Lauren's game was trial and error; having discovered the secrets of top spin, volley, and lob, he employed them with the zeal of the self-educated.

They were sweating lightly, and almost ready. The kids began to gather at the fence. This was the best game in town. He had forgotten when the kids first started coming. Then it had been to gibe and rag at the players: Hey, man, the sport of queens. Hey, man, can't you hit no fuckin' harder? Curious, in a match between a black man and a white man, no racial comments. But, then, he never thought of Lauren as black or himself as white. Lauren's skin was more the color of maple syrup; his—what?—the cement of the pavement? The kids soon settled down, and though one played a ghetto box at its tone-killing peak, they did not distract him.

Spector's game had grown from the clay courts of the Pennsylvania club where he'd worked as a boy. Weeding the courts in the muggy summer air once a week, then swabbing off the night's moisture and rolling them with the drum you filled from the hose. Daily they had to be lined, and he would fill the ancient marker with lime and water, run twine for a guide, and mark off the stripes. There his tennis developed as an exercise of the mind as much as of the body. Lauren hadn't yet learned how to jam the chop player with a serve into the body, to force him to pop the ball up, leaving it exposed to the intercept volley.

The first set went in a now familiar pattern. He controlled the court, and was able to upset Lauren's intensity by varying the pace. His returns, a range of offspeeds, fell by the baseline. This day he broke serve twice, as Lauren double-faulted into the net to cede points. He won, six–three.

They rested on the courtside bench, looking across the Park at the battery of apartments on Fifth. Both swigged from a half-gallon jug of iced tea he had brought.

"Want a tip?"

"No thanks."

"Get your second serve in first."

His opponent arose, wiped his mouth with his forearm and his arm with a towel.

"Want a tip?"

"Sure."

"Watch your ass."

Lauren took nothing off his serves in the next set, and faulted away two games. But something else was happening. When he received service, he had found a new vigor. He returned the ball with intent. And as they played he seemed to realize that Spector's backhand, hit decisively with a two-handed grip, had no dynamics. It deflected the ball accurately, but with a constant and unnotable speed. More and more often, Lauren's play was to that backhand, deeper, heavier. And the backhand faltered, so that its shots began to fall close to the service box.

Gradually the lines of power drew clear. It was as in the mid-game of chess, where, though no pieces fall, the advance of officers and control of diagonals presage a conclusion. The one man quick afoot, gracefully returning shots, the other advancing, leaning into the decelerating strokes, gaining the advantage of geometry. As the darker man foreshortened the court, he increased his choice of response and the obliquity of angle. Lauren won the second set seven games to five.

They sat again on the bench and finished the iced tea. One of the neighborhood kids hung on the mesh behind them.

"Hey, you gonna whup the Man?"

"I'm gonna try, brother."

The kid let out a squeal, a war whoop, and the two players exchanged a smile.

A sense of ineluctability hung over the third set. He battled Lauren to two all; still, he knew his points had come from reservoirs of luck or artifice. In the fifth game Spector executed several first serves, and each came back at him with no more arc than a guy wire. Lauren served for the match and won it at six–two.

Now they sat outside the fence on the grass, resting. Sweat poured through their shirts. A young couple in spotless tennis whites hit back and forth in uneven parabolas. Lauren had bought four bottles of soda pop from a pushcart vendor, and they drank them off.

"You play good."

"I played good today."

He wondered if Lauren realized how tired he was. That's as good as I'll ever be.

"How's the insurance business?" Spector's question was an idle one.

"Reinsurance, man. Can't you get it?"

"Reinsurance. I don't know what it is, is why I can't get it."

"It's a license to mint dough."

They had spoken of it before. Lauren was an accountant. He'd done his undergraduate and graduate work at night. All the while he worked for a reinsurance company, the kind that arranges risk spreads for the major carriers. As he explained it to Spector, there was virtually no risk left over after they got finished arranging, only significant fees. And it was a closed club. You needed a New York State license, and there were none to be had. To break into the business, a new entry has to buy an existing charter.

And that, as Lauren pointed out, took money. And raising money took connections. Spector couldn't tell at first: did Lauren want advice on how to raise the money? Spector felt awkward about giving counsel, thought it might sound patronizing, and avoided it by explaining his antic retirement.

Spector sat, thinking. How many tennis matches had he won and lost? He had played in the number-one slot as a junior on his college team. Before that, high school, camp, tryouts, tournaments. Club matches, Central Park. Two hundred matches? Five hundred? Five thousand? Who will keep his statistics if he disappears? Which of us gets a scrapbook if we don't keep it ourselves? This man, about whom he knew nothing except his locus at a weekly rendezvous and his sizzling forehand, had beaten him in as good a duel as he had had. Perhaps today was the finals, the last bracket for another persona he could now retire.

"Lauren, where do you live?"

A second personal question. He noted the pause.

"Why?"

"I mean, around here?"

"Yeah. Just up the Drive. Why?"

Resolve comes in the morning. He had not yet committed himself, but it was time.

"Look. I'm going to ask you a favor. Say no if it's no."

"Go ahead."

"I live at Eighty-fourth and the Park. I may be taking a trip. I wonder if you'd, say, come by once a week. Pick up my mail. Leave some trash. Make it look as if someone lives there. You know, so I don't get ripped off."

His partner hesitated.

"I'd expect to pay. Say, a hundred a month, for six months. In advance."

"You gettin' ripped off already. You going for six months?"

"I might be. Look, I don't have anyone else I can ask."

Lauren preferred them to remain tennis adversaries. Spector understood. He too liked to confine his relationships. "That's all?"

"That's it. And maybe mail letters for me. My bills. I'll write out the checks in advance. Rent, Con Ed, phone. I'll put them in envelopes. Every month you just mail a set."

"Sounds easy."

"Piece of cake."

"Sure. When you going?"

"I don't know. I may not. I'll tell you next week." He got up to leave, and placed the pop bottles by a wire trash basket where they could be retrieved for the deposit.

"You'll be here next week?" Lauren asked.

"I be here, man. I whup you ass."

He was still sweating as he toweled off from the shower, this time not from exertion but from the hothouse humidity. The air conditioner was a window unit. Its constant noise made it difficult to hear any solos on the stereo that weren't horns, and its main function was reinforcement rather than comfort, for, bolted to the ledge from the inside, it presented an impassable obstacle to one of the four windows. The other three were secured only by grime and the paucity of the interior.

He microwaved some pancakes, slid them onto the plate as the water came to a boil, and sat down to the Saturday *Times*. Flimsy. Nothing in it. The puzzle contained a seven-word synonym for "a masque, a fraud." He filled in "charade," scraped the uneaten glob into the disposal, and ran hot water to course off the extra syrup. Ought to get back into shape, he thought. I might have had that last set. His body remained that of a runner: slight build, developed thighs and calves, narrow upper torso. Not much extra weight. Start eating right again. He pinched his sides through the cotton shirt, and was not unsatisfied with the meager flesh he picked up. Curious, he thought, how we need to show ourselves to advantage. Even when alone.

He arranged his notes on the card table in the living room and pulled up the apartment's only upholstered chair. It was a Georgian reproduction, a wing chair with a light-rose brocade. He visualized its purchase from the auction of a failed midtown hotel where middle managers took their secretaries for affairs, where couples came on matinee theatre packages. It was that heritage he enjoyed. While the chair had seen life, most of it was seamy and unimaginative.

It took him a moment to get into character. He had thought through how to play Roger Weedman. Formal, polite but not obsequious, and—in keeping with his scholastic bent—an Anglophile. With apprehension, he dialed the Lake Forest number.

"Hello."

"Hello, is Mr. Parish in?"

"Yes. He is. That's me."

The voice was that of an older man, a man unused to or uninterested in telephone conventions. But its tone was hale and open.

"Mr. Parish. Glad I caught you. Roger Weedman here." Spector's pulse began to race, and he took a breath and blew out, as he would for an important second serve.

"Who? Do I know you?"

Parish sounded as if he wanted to.

"Roger Weedman, Mr. Parish. The chap who wrote about watching over your house."

A moment of silence. He wasn't sure he had the nerves for this new life.

"Oh, yes. Sure. Well. How are you, Mr. Weedman?"

"I'm very well, Mr. Parish. And how are you?"

"I'm splendid, young man. Nice of you to call."

"I'm glad to hear that, sir. I'm glad to hear you're splendid. I'm calling to suggest we meet. When you're in New York next week."

"Good idea. Why?"

"To discuss the house. Whether I'm acceptable to you."

"For the house?"

"Yes. For the house."

Had he lost out? Was his first real prospect infirm of mind?

"Roger Weedman, I like your thinking. Now, to tell you the truth, we didn't have a rental in mind. We had in mind more of a house sitter."

"That would be wonderful."

Spector didn't need the free ride, but it would reduce the dollars at risk. He knew he might need a second chance for this scheme, and a second grubstake to finance it.

"It's a service to us, you understand. See, we have cats. And Lila, that's my bride, Lila just hates to board them when we travel. They never forgive you. Would you mind watching the cats?"

It was a subject on which he had forgotten to prepare.

"I don't know much about them, Mr. Parish. What's involved?"

"Involved? Why, there's damn little. They go out and in. They're not involved. Simplicity itself. We leave food and water. They go out and in by themselves, you see. Now, they do like conversation."

"Any particular subjects?"

"Not that I can determine. Mostly the sound of your voice."

Spector was smiling, and though he had no hint of inflection he thought the man on the end of the line was too.

"Where are you staying, Mr. Parish?"

"Why, where we always do. We always stay at the Pierre. We don't like those chains."

"The Pierre. Shall I meet you there, then? You get in on a Thursday. How about eight-thirty Friday morning."

"That's a dandy idea. We'll have breakfast. They have a nice room for breakfast."

Spector confirmed time and date once more, unsure as to whether the information had registered.

"Oh, Mr. Weedman."

"Yes?"

"We checked with your college."

"So you said in the letter."

"They think you live in Houston."

An easy one. He had studied for worse.

"I'm glad you reminded me, Mr. Parish. No wonder I haven't been getting my alumni magazine. That Houston address is years out of date."

They rang off cordially.

Spector shrugged off the vigorous sets of the morning. Newly resolved, he lay down, propped himself up on his neck and shoulders, and proceeded through ten minutes of fevered bicycling. He took the second shower of the day ice-cold.

5

Spector was stumped. He stared at the chart on the wall. There was one problem he could not solve.

This scheme could net a pile of money. Many a sound plan

had faltered, not in its execution, but in the reintroduction of the loot. This money had to be cleaned. For that process he would need time, to develop a mechanism, to file income-tax returns and pay the taxes. Once the money had passed through the elaborate gymkhana of the Internal Revenue Service, it was ready to come into the market. Legal tender, as they say.

Though he had never done it, that process—washing, as the popular press called it—was within his ken. But in the meantime he would be a fugitive. Law enforcement would be looking for him, and after that whoever carried the insurance for the damaged bank. For that interlude, he needed an identity to succeed Roger Weedman.

And Spector knew what every movie fan knows. Like clarets, fugitives from abroad are a better class. The domestic ones, Cagney and John Garfield, hid out in trailer parks. Abroad were Cary Grant in Monaco, Guinness in Rio. The criminal's life abroad required a facility for languages and a white dinner jacket. Spector owned both. Without significant difficulty, he decided that after the check cleared he would be bound overseas.

There lay his problem: how does one get a false passport? Nothing in his education or experience had prepared him. The commodity must exist, and like all commodities it must have an established market. As he knew from the films, in Marseilles or Morocco it would have been easy. You found suppliers by speaking out on a street corner. But in the middle of Manhattan, and in particular his Manhattan, he lived, he had discovered, in his peculiar caste. His access to contraband was restricted. He could within minutes purchase high-grade cocaine, or information on a merger that would not be public until tomorrow's *Journal*. But—since he had done neither he couldn't be sure—those sources were as remote as he from an illegal gun, the name of an arsonist, or a forged passport.

And so, on a pleasant morning in late summer, Spector dressed in a gray twill shirt, arms torn off at the shoulder seams, and his only pair of jeans, and descended into the subway bound for Queens. Not merely Queens, but Jackson Heights: that section where, his studies of Jimmy Breslin had assured him, the Family ruled and prospered.

It was almost eleven. He could hear the apprehension in his

ears. It rang like static and crowded out other sounds, so that even the crash of the cars as they rolled into the IRT station was tolerable.

Spector let the first train go by. He hadn't thought this through. He understood risks of the mind and purse but not of the body. He had no interest in jeopardizing his health, and this particular masquerade would take him into a neighborhood where he was irrefutably a fraud. Though he had worn and washed the shirt twice, his clothes looked implausibly new. His shoulders stuck out, white and conspicuous.

Behind him the wall had been freshly crayoned with graffiti. Slyly he backed against it. Swaying to imaginary music, he rubbed grime onto his shirt. Later, as the train rushed through the darkness of the tunnel under the East River, he would transfer dirt to his front and arms. Every actor learns there are roles for which the costuming comes hard.

The ride took twenty minutes. No one paid him much mind, and he began to calm down with the realization that his motives were not written on his face. He walked up the steps and out the faded wooden kiosk into the sun.

He found himself on a broad street with two-way traffic. The buildings were red brick. Upstairs were apartments with white cotton curtains that blew out into the sun. Downstairs, small retail stores: appliances, zapatería, two beauty salons, liquor, an employment agency. People—Spanish, black, Anglo—walked leisurely on ancient sidewalks amid larches going into seed. It was twenty minutes and five miles from Manhattan, but it was connected to the Manhattan Spector knew only by those fragile dimensions of time and space. Nowhere to be seen was a tie, a pair of high heels, a yellow pad, a *New York Times*. As Spector passed, two old men chatted idly while their leashed dogs defecated, rear to rear, in the gutter.

He walked three blocks and passed several bars. The first, he decided, looked most promising. "Sullivan's" was written in neon script over the façade, and on the plate-glass window was painted a four-leaf clover. Spector's source for information was an old friend who had told him once, at a dinner party, about the Family and its connections in the business world: fruit and vegetables, coin machines, saloons. He and Joan had speculated whether the fellow was mostly hot air. Now he was in Queens on the strength of that idle chatter, having decided that finding a bar was easier than asking his neighborhood grocer. He was no longer sure.

He opened the door of Sullivan's and gazed into the blackness. He saw nothing. Standing at the very gates of hell without a guide, he wondered, for the first time since he had decided to go forward, whether the wiser choice would not be to call the executive recruiter whose card he had thrown into his top dresser drawer.

Even as he considered, his eyes widened to the softening darkness. Now he made out two men. One, tall and wearing a white shirt and apron, was leaning on the bar, filling in some sort of form. At the far end, for the bar ran the length of the room, sat a second man, his chin on his palm, contemplating two glasses in front of him.

"Help you?"

"Yeah," Spector said, entering. "A beer."

"Wha' kind?"

"Whadd'ya got on tap?"

"Schaeffer's."

"Do fine."

Spector pulled out a stool so that the two customers were equidistant from the spigots, and sat down. The door swung closed behind him, and he was left to fend in the crepuscular light from the beer signs and video machines. The mixture was a soft green glow, making the faces look purposefully discolored. The tones, the texture rang a familiar note in Spector's memory. That was the light Titian had used on the dead Christ.

A glass of beer was set in front of him on a saturated napkin.

"Can I get a sandwich?"

The bartender looked at him. Clearly the wrong question.

"Only microwave," he said. "Ham, ham and cheese, meatball. Also nachos."

"Ham and cheese. Be fine."

The man nodded, retrieved a cellophane package from a subcounter refrigerator, placed it in the oven, and punched the buttons. Spector had misinterpreted his nervousness as hunger. Now he would have to eat whatever it was he had ordered.

The sandwich came.

"Seventy and one fifty," the bartender said. "Two twenty."

Spector pulled a wallet from his hip and took out a fifty.

"I have to break that?"

31

"Maybe not," Spector said. It didn't register.

"Maybe you can help me." He looked meaningfully at the man, but still got no reaction.

"How do you go about getting a passport?"

"You mean the whiskey?"

"No. A passport, identification. How would I buy one?"

"Mister, this is a bar." The bartender wrinkled his nose. The third man spoke up.

"You don't buy those. You *get* 'em. The government gives 'em to you."

"That's right," said the bartender. "Carl's right."

Spector went along.

"Gives it to you?"

"Sure. My sister has one. For travel and shit like that. Tell you what you do. You know where Montauk Street is?"

"No," said Spector.

"You go out here to the left. Two blocks is all. Montauk. Right across that intersection is a police station. They'll give you one. You need a picture, though."

His trip so far had cost Spector two twenty and an entire morning. Plus subway fare. He needed to give this one more try.

"I don't want my own," he explained. "I want somebody else's."

"Can't do that," Carl explained. "You gotta get your own. They won't give you somebody else's. That's what you need the picture for."

"Oh." Spector looked down and saw his fifty-dollar bill lying on the bar.

"I may have something smaller." The bartender nodded with slight satisfaction. Spector replaced the bill with a five, and the bartender took it to the register for change.

"Here you go."

"Thanks."

Spector pocketed the change and began to eat his sandwich.

"Hey," said Carl to no one. "How 'bout those Mets."

"Goddamn," said Spector, his mouth full. "How 'bout them?"

He hailed a cab and gave the driver destination and route. It's the time of day, Spector explained. The Fifty-ninth Street Bridge was a better choice. The driver made no response.

Spector had grown up in Wilkes-Barre, a small city in north-eastern Pennsylvania. Classmates at college used to tell Spector that it was a depressed area, but he didn't believe it: at either end of a depression is an elevation and, in Spector's memory and his parents', prosperity had never visited. His father's father had worked at construction, had helped build the bridge over the Susquehanna, his mother's father raised poultry and, when that didn't pay, ran ovens in the brickyards. No one in the family worked at the town's dreariest industry, the anthracite mines, but the grime it produced had shaded their lives.

In the summer the heat gathered among the rounded hills like dust, and in winter the cold, sinking air seeped through the valleys. Spector remembered the intermediary seasons, those of the equinox, as temperate and lovely, but they were brief. Downtown there were retail stores on the main street that had been boarded up since he could recall.

His parents both taught at a local high school. Her subject was biology and his civics. They had met at a state teachers' college nearby, and returned to their hometown after the Second World War. Spector was their only child, and they had pinned on him their most futile hopes and, inextricably, their most severe frustrations.

They both hoped for a change in the social order. A peaceful change. His father's hero was John Stuart Mill. By the time Mill was eight he had read Xenophon and Herodotus, and Spector, dawdling through comic books, disappointed early.

At the dinner table his father used to instruct him on the necessity of understanding the capitalist system in order to change it. Spector liked Mill's arguments. By its own momentum the system will evolve into something better. Mill saw property as a device of an older society, necessary to achieve stability but now an atavism, the very weight which, when transferred from the base of the column to its capital, would overturn the institution of society itself.

And Spector's father argued that the intelligentsia could see this today. But in the fifth decade of the twentieth century, he would say, the intelligent are powerless to change it. They had not prepared themselves, entering teaching and the professions instead of commerce and banking. If you want to change the system, his father would say, you must be inside it.

Although they never acknowledged it, Spector became an

accomplished student. True, he never caught up to J. S. Mill. He went through college on full scholarship. Many of his classmates, in fervent dedication to a better world, thought him a philistine when, as his parents had hoped, he entered business.

He was convinced that, for the most part, his father was wrong. The intelligentsia were not likely to foretell the changes in the world because they didn't play in the world. They weren't at the table. But in one narrower view his father had been right. To use the system, you must know it. Banking and money to a socialist would be like anatomy to a surgeon. Once credentialed, Spector had no interest in becoming an agent of change. Rather, he admired what he saw, the elegant trappings that concealed the bloody hooves of natural selection. He understood the urge of the greatest exponents of the system to play with its odds, to expound free enterprise on the one hand while working on the other to assure nepotism, government protection, clubby cartel. He gradually came to realize that those who did best at it, even those who did so legally, had a healthy streak of anarchy. For, if success were the most important rule, everything else was a venal ordinance.

As the taxi sped across the bridge, he struck up a conversation with the driver.

"They say New York cabbies get asked everything."

"Oh, yes, sir." He was a Pakistani. Spector had asked. An amiable fellow who watched Spector in the rearview mirror as if his passenger might be armed.

"Well, tell me, Mobullah," reading his name from the hack license on display, "where would you go about getting a fake passport?"

"In Karachi no problem. But it is expensive. Several thousand rupees when I was there. My cousin uses one to go to Vancouver. You know Vancouver?"

"What about New York? How would you get one in New York?"

"I don't need one, thank you. My passport is authentic. And I have green card."

They sped across the Park at Eighty-sixth. Out of caution, Spector had given him the address of the Beresford, two blocks from where he lived. Mobullah was a skillful driver, impeded by no fear of vehicle, pedestrian, or orthodoxy.

34

"How would I get one, Mo? If I wanted one?"

"Oh, I do not know, sir." They pulled up and Spector waved off the oncoming doorman. "But I can tell you this."

"Yes?" Spector said expectantly. Mo made change and waited for his tip.

"It is illegal. You better watch out. In Pakistan no one cares. But I think here it is different."

He walked to the post office to check the Weedman mail drop. He had to wait until two girls before him, in halters and fake leather skirts, opened their box. Something good had arrived, and they chattered excitedly as they tore the envelope.

"Excuse me," he said finally. They went off without acknowledging him, arm in arm, reading aloud.

He opened the metal door and smiled at what he saw. Four pieces of mail. It had to be good news. He scanned the return addresses. All commercial; no more responses for house sitting. When he had mailed off the credit-card applications, he had no banking information to give, and so he listed only his post-office box and the names of the other card companies as credit references. The first of his applications had passed. The envelope he opened contained a letter from a gasoline company, welcoming him to their family of customers, and enclosing duplicate cards for himself and his spouse.

The other mail was a product of the first letter. The gasoline company had evidently sold Weedman's name on their mailing list. Intimations of immortality. Weedman had a solicitation to buy ten thousand dollars' worth of term insurance without a medical, to get a set of coins with the likeness of U.S. presidents, and, on the strength of any other card, to get a thousand dollars' credit at one of the major banks in the city. He filled out this last application, folded it into the metered envelope, and mailed it. The rest he discarded.

His Roger Weedman was beginning to assemble an identity. The process was not dissimilar to that of a giant reflector telescope as it gathers inscrutable glimmers of light and pools them until they can be said to yield, not a star, but the image of a star. And the image of a person is all I need for this first try. This first conceit.

Spector had not been very adept at the study of sciences at school. He was always more interested in the way information

35

came to people than in what it was. He was especially fond of the tale of the Göttigen astronomer Carl Freidrich Gauss, who constructed a curve for recording a series of observations of the heavens. Gauss realized that each observation contains error, and that we base our knowledge on those errors. The Gausstian curve tells us how those errors scatter on a spectrum. What we say we know merely lies in the area of least uncertainty, reality merely the suspicion we share. That illusion is all that Spector hoped for.

6

The great New York hotels, Spector considered as he entered the Pierre that morning, suffer a terrible insecurity. They model themselves either on Edwardian England, like the Carlyle with its white-gloved livery and its disdain for commercialism, or on the French monarchy. The Pierre followed the second school. Not surprising. At these prices, it's a good bet that damn few of their guests favor the populist causes.

He walked through the lobby to the curved stairwell that descended to the breakfast room. Gilded ogee moldings traced the walls. The effect was of an eighteenth-century Parisian townhouse, despoiled only by modern necessities: telephones buzzing and large window-advertisements in the niches instead of statuary. Because of a famous robbery several years back, the entire front desk was enclosed in a thick Plexiglass shield.

He had dressed with some care. When he was commuting downtown, Spector had been conscious of style, and his shirts and suits had been made by two firms of tailors. It was another excess that he had picked up like a burr and never thought to discard. And though he was not short of clothes, he had none to emulate those of a struggling academician. This morning he chose a pair of lightweight khaki trousers he'd never worn to work, with a blue blazer. To give his dress that slight discordant note he thought bespoke good scholarship, he picked out a wool knit tie, ill suited to New York summers.

Ready for his first performance, Spector entered the dining room and stopped by the lectern. The maître d'hôtel was walking quickly toward him across the room, holding up a finger to signal him to wait.

"Table for one?"

"I'm joining Mr. and Mrs. Parish. Are they here?"

The maître d' eyed his outfit with displeasure.

"Yes. Of course. Come this way,"

The room was busy. Spector was ambivalent about crossing the open room. On the one hand, this hotel was a show-business favorite, and if there were celebrities to be spotted at breakfast, he didn't want to miss them. On the other, the Pierre was a popular choice for high-level business breakfasts, and he must avoid running into former colleagues. He followed the back of the head in front of him.

Seated by the kitchen door, doubtless also disfavored by their appearance, was a couple. The man rose to shake his hand.

"Mr. Weedman? I'm Edgar Parish."

Parish wore a silk jacket, pale lemon, and an open-collared white knit shirt. Spector shook his hand over the table.

"And this is my bride, Lila."

They were both a well-fed, well-tanned sixty. Lila Parish had gray hair and glass-gray eyes. In Spector's mind to her credit, she wore only the faintest brush strokes of makeup on lips and brow. She looked directly at him to say hello, and he liked her at once.

Her husband seemed to have none of her assurance. He was eager to please, and talked nervously about their room and

37

the items on the menu. Parish was flushed, and the color of his pate matched the redness of his face, although, Spector guessed, from different sources. Several capillaries around his nostrils had enlarged, showing a blue lacework. Spector waited for him to suggest a Bloody Mary. He didn't.

"Well, now, Roger. You're living in New York."

Despite his immersion in the role, Spector was not prepared to hear himself called by another's name. He stammered.

"That's right, Mr. Parish. I moved from Houston several years ago. The research facilities are superb here. I've been able to get most of my book work behind me."

"I suppose. You can't get me to stay here more than I have to. Now, mind you, New York's got lots of things. But I don't do research and I'm too old to chase skirts." Here he winked and patted his wife's hand. "No, I'd rather stay home and play golf."

"That's directed at me, Roger," Mrs. Parish said with good nature. "I'm dragging Edgar off for two months in Europe, away from his beloved game."

"Not so, Sweetie. I get to play twice in Scotland."

He patted her again. Clearly there had been a negotiation. Mrs. Parish's hand was that of an older woman, freckled with liver spots. It bore enough stone and metal to pass for a Fabergé egg.

They ordered. Parish and his wife treated the young man as if he were a visiting collegian, the son of a good friend. Spector had to remind himself that his plot would do them no harm at all. Mild embarrassment and perhaps some lost time, but no damage. Besides, they'd get five years' dinner-table talk for their troubles. He smiled at Lila, more than a little sad as he imagined her describing him as "such a nice boy too." Their breakfasts arrived.

"Don't you love this dining room?" Mrs. Parish asked. "It's so cozy. Makes me want to redo our old house."

"It's interesting," Spector said.

"What would you call this architecture? French provincial?"

Mr. Parish was salting his omelet, marmalading his toast, all with an animation that took him out of the conversation.

"No. More rococo, I think."

"Rococo," Mrs. Parish said. She liked the word. It would go back to Illinois with her.

"At its best the rococo was a reaction. Like the baroque. Builders got tired of symmetry and stability. They wanted to break out of the classic, the plain surfaces, the masses that looked like mass. So"—here Spector pointed with his butter knife to the arch over the swinging doors to the kitchen—"so they twisted columns, they carved or fluted architraves. They stopped cornices midway."

Mrs. Parish followed his hand. Mr. Parish sipped his coffee.

"It was a product of boredom," Spector continued. "They'd been doing one thing too long. Needed a change."

"That's a legitimate motive, Mr. Weedman. Don't you agree?" she asked in a maternal voice. She wanted concord.

"Oh, I do. And please call me Roger."

"And you must call us by our first names too. If you're going to be our house sitter."

The best way to land the job was to be pursued. Eventually to be convinced.

He straightened up to signal that business could now be discussed. "Well," he said. "Let's talk about that, shall we? I'd like to know what you have in mind."

Edgar Parish responded. "You bet. We're gone two months. Back October 22. We have a house in Lake Forest. Not too large. Grounds. Nothing for you to do outside, though. Man comes in once a week, gardener. Cleans up, does the pool and Jacuzzi, that sort of thing."

Parish had an odd way with fricatives. A trace of lisp. One couldn't mimic that voice easily.

"I need quiet for my work, Edgar."

"This is quiet. Out in the country. Used to be country, until they subdivided so much of it."

"You've had the house a long time?"

"My father built it in 1936. Right in the middle of the Depression. I hate to tell you what it cost him. Peanuts. Nobody stood on ceremony about unions then. All happy to have the work."

"There is one thing," Lila said apprehensively.

They waited. Spector couldn't guess.

"We have cats. Five of them. Would you mind?"

"What would I have to do?"

"Oh, you don't have to *do* anything. Their food is out."

"For two months?"

39

"It's on a timer. And Norton, that's the gardener, he'll check to see it's working. And there's water. And they use the pet door to go potty."

Spector nodded. The euphemism had discomfited him, but he tried to keep a straight face. The conversation stopped, and Spector cut his bacon.

"Now, we don't see any need for rent." Edgar wanted to close the deal. "We fly out tonight, and we'd just leave you the keys, and our travel schedule, and you could get there whenever you like. We left kinda hoping we could get you to watch it for us. Norton knows you might be coming."

Spector said nothing. Parish went on.

"We'd feel better if someone were living there. Not that it's dangerous, you understand. But you know, these days. We'd just feel better. Especially if it was you, Roger. Somebody writing a book. Lila's a great reader."

"Is that so?"

"Yes," she said, embarrassed. "I read everything Jeffrey Archer writes. Not what you'd be writing though. About architecture."

"History."

"History," confirmed Edgar. "We'd sure feel better. Incidentally, who is it you're writing about? I know I've heard of him."

"Charlemagne," Spector said with disappointment. He had slogged through that biography.

He was close to the balance point. To that imperceptible locus in the negotiation where there was little territory left to gain. He had a favorite metaphor for the commercial relationship—Joan had said, for every relationship—as a tug of war on a plateau. You had to pull and pull, to gain as large a slice as possible of the other fellow's territory by pulling, without backing up so far you fell off.

The Parishes were giving ground easily. There were a few more feet to be had.

"It sounds interesting. The cats won't bother me, and neither will Norton, I'm sure. I'm really quite a hermit. Norton might not ever see me.

"But I *am* conscientious. If I'm to be your tenant, your house sitter for two months, it's like"—and, conscious of furrowing his brow, he searched for the apt simile—"it's like being a trust officer."

They nodded in earnest.

"And I'll want the telephone numbers of people I might need."

"You mean the police or the vet? They're written right next to the phone in the kitchen."

"Good. Also, your children's names. The names of your doctor, lawyer, banker."

"Gracious, why?" Lila asked.

"Well, if anything goes wrong. If you have a car accident and I need to get your records abroad. Or if you need to get money abroad and you can't call when the bank's open."

His solicitude pleased them.

"That's easy enough." Edgar had the waiter bring him pencil and pad and began writing.

"Do these people know you're away?"

"Our son and his wife do. That's our only family. They would have come to stay in the house, but school's starting for their kids."

"And the others?" Spector indicated the list.

"Good heavens, no. My bank knows too much about me already. And I can't afford to tell our lawyer. Now, if something *does* happen," Edgar said softly, "you don't have to worry. The law firm has our wills, and John Dixon, that's with the bank, has a list of all our stuff. Copies of the trusts, the whole shee-bang."

Parish would likely tell him everything he needed to know, he'd fill in the forms, if Spector could last through two more cups of coffee. But a tocsin sounded in his invisible ear. Time to close the deal.

"Well," he said, satisfied. "Edgar and Lila, it sounds like just the place. I know I'll be able to do a lot of work there."

The Parishes were genuinely pleased. As was he. He reached for the bill, displaying the Weedman credit card he had felt so fortunate to get. Parish protested, took the check from him, and signed it. They sat for minutes more while Lila explained the household appliances, and Edgar wrote out directions and the code and telephone number for the security system. At Spector's suggestion, he also wrote and signed a letter identifying Weedman as an authorized occupant of the house.

41

"Roger, dear," Lila was saying, "we didn't leave many perishables. The market's only two miles down the road, you'll see it. And the pantry is full, and there are steaks and chops and hams in the freezer. Not the small one in the kitchen, but the large one in the guest rooms over the garage. And that dreadful venison that Edgar brings back from Quebec every year. The duck we're saving for Christmas has a label on it."

"Help yourself to the liquor cabinet," Edgar said. "Whatever else you need, ask Norton." Spector needed to end the conversation. Their consideration was burying him.

"I'm sure it'll be just fine. You go off and don't worry."

They left him with two sets of house keys. The car keys were on the pegboard in the pantry, the TV remote control in the nightstand in the master bedroom. They shook hands. He wished them *bon voyage*.

Joan had not understood. It was not winning that he cared about. And it was surely not money. It was, if a word could be found, distinction. Spector saw the world as a spiritually crowded place, where one needed to attain a certain height of ego to breathe. His parents nurtured only the conventional dreams, even down to their desire to see him succeed, and he early fastened on this need for a space set apart. The antic, the eccentric helped get him there. The ordinary dragged him down.

It was a meaning of "distinction" Joan did not admit to, and she confused his with the more common neurosis.

"Just like you said in Group that day," she would tell him, "you have to win."

But Joan didn't understand. That wasn't it at all.

In the months before the divorce, Joan had suggested a marriage counselor, who in turn suggested they join a weekly session of foundering couples like themselves. Group, they called it. They both disliked the sessions, in which everyone was expected to bare his discontent and, for the first time in Spector's experience, incivility was the goal. Nonetheless, they went regularly. Logic dictated that they take some measure to save their marriage, and they were, after all, devotees of logic. The advantage of this particular step, they both agreed, was that it required only their presence.

At one Group, the counselor had introduced the topic of money. People had different views of it, she said, and it would help to hear how different they were. For instance, she said in her intensive-care-ward voice, how much money do we need? We work hard for it. Have we ever sat back and asked ourselves how much we would need?

She asked Spector to start, since most of the time he was lugubrious and detached.

"I'll have to think about that," he said. "Go to someone else."

And so they went around the room. Joan said, Enough to be happy. And she thought she had enough. No one pointed out the contradiction. A woman who bought gloves and purses for Bergdorf's said a million in the bank. A real-estate lawyer talked about returns on investment and the federal funds rate. Someone said whatever they paid his boss. They came back to Spector.

"All right. Your turn. To be happy, how much would you need?"

"All of it," he said.

7

The Parishes were to check out that very afternoon for the night flight to Charles DeGaulle. Spector waited impatiently. He broke up the time by shopping. At a discount store on Forty-seventh, he bought a telephone-answering machine with a remote unit. Then he walked across to Madison and up to Paul Stuart, where he bought a yellow silk sports jacket, a white knit shirt, and a white patent-leather belt. The only tennis shirts he owned bore identifying club or school insignias. He could use this one even after he retired the character.

The staging costs of the production had just taken a leap forward. He didn't want an extended run. The jacket was to be ready in five days, and he agreed to pick it up, leaving the name of Roger Weedman and a false address.

He stopped by the United Airlines office at the corner of Forty-eighth and Fifth and purchased a round-trip ticket for Chicago, again in Weedman's name. For all purchases he paid cash. Tempting as it was to try his new credit cards, the idea struck him as felonious. He made himself unpopular at a bank by changing forty dollars into quarters.

Back at the apartment, he stored his silver in an empty tennis-ball can. It was the weight of a shot put. Still the time crept by. He called Lauren to cancel Saturday's game.

"You don't take losing well."

"Sorry, Lauren. Have to be out of town."

"You want me to start watching your place?"

"No. I'll be back before the long trip."

"All right. Later."

"See you."

Spector's nerves were beginning to rumble like a power mower in heavy grass. He turned on the stereo and chose a record he could listen to with one ear. Solo Monk. He made the next call with apprehension, even though he knew there was no risk.

"I'm sorry. Mr. Parish has checked out. We could forward a message."

"No need. Thanks."

Spector pulled out the results of his research on banks. Inside a large manila jacket were notes on the Standard & Poor's Banking Digest. He had written out the standards of measurement. It was not unlike finding a good merger candidate for a client. Asset size, single- or holding-company bank, national versus state charter.

Economics and speed limited his choices to the New York metropolitan area. Also, the bank must be one that would consider a sizable signature loan neither extraordinary nor beyond lending capacity. He didn't want to bear the scrutiny of a second, participating bank. That suggested a large asset base. But the chosen bank should feel flattered, should want the business. At best, it would be able to move fast, would be so hungry to land the customer that it would cut a few corners. That suggested an autonomous bank, not one of a great chain like the prominent money-center institutions. Finally they had to be lean. A high ratio of assets to employees. A young loan officer, itching to use all his responsibility, eager to move up fast.

The notes in front of him showed his process. They ranked all Manhattan banks of suitable size. Those with holding-company affiliations had been crossed out. He had ranked the rest by recent growth and size of staff. After checking the list of officers and eliminating two banks that employed acquaintances, he had come down to two top choices—he believed in a redundancy—Gramercy National and Empire State.

He dialed Gramercy's number and, with the copied page from S & P in front of him, asked by name for the vice-president of personal lending.

"I'm sorry. He's in a meeting. May I help you."

"Yes. My name is Parish. I'm in from Chicago for the day, and I should like to establish banking relationships here in New York."

"You wish to open an account."

"I wish to talk about a line of credit. For investments."

"That would be Mr. Mulroy in personal banking. I'll put you through."

Spector waited. Over the receiver, the Ray Coniff singers sang to him. "Blueberry Hill." It drowned out Monk's piano.

Some world, he thought. What I'm doing is a felony. Muzak is legal.

"Mulroy."

"Mr. Mulroy. My name is Edgar Parish. I'm from Lake Forest. In for the day. Staying at the Pierre."

The technique was the creation of an archetype through proper nouns. Shakespeare did it best.

"I'm looking for a bank to use for some local investing I may be doing."

"Yes?"

"That is your business, isn't it?"

"I beg your pardon."

Spector drew a line on the pad through Gramercy National.

"Your business. Making loans."

"Yes, it is."

"Would you be interested in another customer?"

"Ah, Mr. Parish." A note of condolence. "We couldn't possiby do anything over the phone."

"I'm not asking you that, Mr. Mulroy. I'm not asking you to *do* anything. I'm asking if you'd like to consider another customer."

"Well, I would suggest, Mr. Parish, that you come in and see us. Make an appointment. We're at 595 Lexington Avenue."

"I know where you are, Mr. Mulroy."

"Very well."

"Good day."

Mulroy, you'll never get the credit you deserve. Perhaps two choices weren't enough.

The switchboard at Empire State rang the senior loan officer. His secretary took the call and directed it elsewhere.

"This is Mr. Urso. Can I help you?"

"I don't know, Mr. Urso. I'm beginning to wonder myself."

Spector turned down the volume on the record and went through his speech. He also toned down his hauteur. He didn't want to go back to the library.

"Mr. Parish," Urso was saying, "you've come to the right place. Empire State wants your business. We're always interested in new business. What size loan did you have in mind?"

"That will depend, Mr. Urso." On what I can find out in Lake Forest, he thought. But all he said was, "I'll have a better fix on that when I come back next week."

"You'll be back? Fine. Otherwise I would suggest your coming in today. If you can't make it in, why, we can use your local bank to do the paperwork for us. Who is that bank?"

Spector gave Urso the name and telephone number Parish had written down for him.

"But I'd rather you wait to call him until I've explained this. You know how people can be when they see a piece of profitable business go elsewhere."

Urso was accommodating. "Absolutely. No fear. I just thought you might be in a rush to get this into the pipeline."

Mr. Urso had a deliciously tough New York accent. Spector wondered if he had come up through the ranks. With that voice, he would make a good undertaker—the department where defaulting loans went to be worked out.

"Well, I would like this to go speedily. Will you be handling it?"

"No, sir. I'm Business Development. My job is to get you in the door. Then I give you over to a loan officer, and their job is to get you the money. We got terrific loan officers, Mr. Parish. You'll love 'em."

Spector was pleased. He thought Parish should be too and should show it.

"Sounds fine. I'll get my papers together. You'll need a financial statement, clearance to call my bank. What else?"

"You know how it is, Mr. Parish. They'll want all the crap, excuse the expression. Name, Social Security, jobs for the last five years, tax returns. They have a loan application long as my arm."

"Tell you what, Mr. Urso. Let's get started. You send it up to my hotel this afternoon. That way I can begin on it. And I'll have it ready when I'm in town next week."

"Great. We'll be talkin' to you, Mr. Parish."

"A pleasure, Mr. Urso."

One last call. Spector reached the concierge at the Pierre and, without identifying himself, informed him that Mr. Parish had left for the airport forgetting that an important envelope was to arrive from Empire State Bank. Would the concierge see that it was forwarded to Mr. Parish's home address? Send it Federal Express and add it to Mr. Parish's bill.

Of course he would.

Spector turned the record volume back up. He strolled around the room, shadow-boxing. He stalked the Queen Anne wing chair and gave it a one-two combination that lifted its front legs off the ground and would have KO'd any lesser chair. He raised his hands in a victory clasp and danced back to a neutral corner.

Pity he didn't have a match with Lauren today. He could vaporize a tennis ball today. Today was his day.

The beauty of the plan, he had thought upon conception, was its single-thread construction. One string. It wasn't like a merger or a tender offer, where, once announced, your motives, identity, temperament were revealed and the opposition began organizing in reaction. The architecture of these early stages he particularly admired, admired the ability at any time to change his mind, pull that single thread, and unravel the entire plan. Fold up the puppet theatre, put the dolls away, and be gone. Parish and his wife would speculate on what had become of that bright young professor who never showed up to house sit. Mr. Urso would realize you can't kiss every pretty girl and cross off the name Parish from his monthly status report to the New Business Committee. The salesman at Paul Stuart would recount how a young Midwesterner had insisted he wanted a white belt to wear with that elegant silk jacket, paid cash for everything, and then never picked up his order.

Escapes at every step. It was more than aesthetics. He was unsure that he would enjoy the life. He had been taught to expect fear and remorse as the autonomous reaction of the moral man to the antisocial act. In his parents' rigorous lessons of societal good, that was what was supposed to happen. Like breaking out in hives.

His parents were not religious. Somewhere in the family there were loose Quaker strains, but it had been beyond memory that any Spector had been to church. No, his parents were lace-curtain socialists, and the brand of ethics they served at his childhood dinner table was that of pragmatism and well-being. Emerson, Aristotle, and, of course, John Stuart Mill. Not good and evil from the Bible. Rather, good as the expression of human structure. John, I think you're going to be disappointed in me.

If you listened to his parents, the moral man can't do wrong because he won't enjoy doing wrong. Spector was disproving their theories. He realized that all the escape hatches he had planned would go unused, that his circumspection was an excess. He had never enjoyed anything more.

He had one more call to make. It was like Shelley to worry over him, especially if he couldn't be found. Shelley liked to keep in touch.

"Well, I think you're nuts. You know what 'bonkers' means?"

Spector was smiling as the conversation began. "Yeah, Shelley. I know."

"At twenty-nine, people don't find themselves. People are already found."

"Thirty-one."

"People who make the kind of money you've made already found themselves. Have you considered that possibility? That the bozo who was knocking down six figures and used to be married to Joan was *you*?"

"Give me a break. No sunrise sermons today. I just wanted to say, if you don't hear from me for a while, don't worry. I'll be on the move. I'll drop you a line."

"You thought any more about what I said? About brass fittings?"

"I have. And thanks. I mean that. But it's not for me."

"Okay, kid. Go find yourself. But let me give you some advice."

"What's that?"

"You find this guy you're looking for, play him some gin. Ten cents a point. He's a real patzer."

Lake Forest

8

He opened the cupboards. It was like coming home. Rich or poor, American householders follow cultural patterns. Here were the soups and there the canned juices and there the specialty items someone had bought on a whim—turtle soup, tinned kippers, a Hawaiian sauce for barbecue. By the spices were stuck the plastic packets that couldn't be thrown out: chicken broth, prizes from cereals, take-out soy sauce. Under the sink, a trash bag, a semicircular scrub brush, rubber gloves. And when, Lila Parish, was the last time you did the dishes?

He had flown out early that day, the last Sunday in August, from a sweltering JFK into the teeth of a rainstorm. The taxi found the turnoff with Spector in the back seat giving instructions from the driver's street map and Edgar Parish's directions. They found Parmalee Road, itself a narrow serpentine that led to a cul-de-sac at the property bordering the lake. The rains made observation difficult. It was like being in a heavily land-scaped car wash. Finally a mail box with Canadian geese in flight and below it "The Parishes" in brass.

They went slowly up the wooded gravel drive. The stones gave a watery sound under the tires. Spector could make out beech, laurel, American elm, and several fruit trees, all dripping and glistening dark green in the downpour.

He stood under a white portico and paid the driver. The

rains had come to end a heat spell, and the earth smelled of the summer. It will be lovely in the fall, he thought, when the Parishes return.

He entered through a Colonial arch. To his surprise, instead of the silence he had prepared himself for, he heard the eerie sound of Edgar Parish, asking someone to leave his name and address at the beep. It was the measured, self-conscious tone, not the words, that put Spector at ease. He found the recording machine in place, and he lifted the receiver as the caller was leaving his message.

"Hello. That's right, but they're away. I don't know how long. They won't be able to come next week for sure. Their house sitter. I certainly will, ma'am."

Reflexively he wrote the woman's name and message. He looked down, crumpled the paper, and threw it away. Must remember to take out the garbage. Then he printed the caller's message. They had few examples of his handwriting. No need to make it easy.

Spector went quickly through the building. It was a handsome house, modern for 1936. Split-level, single-story. The suburban brick ranch house. The best, and probably among the prototypes, of a style grown common by its repetition. But original when built, and today sound and useful in a peculiarly American brand of utility. The rooms lay out simply, interconnected with a sturdy common sense. Fine materials, the stone in the floor, the hardwoods over the mantel and in the bare beams, the slate in the kitchen. Expensive, honest, durable.

The house sprawled into two wings. To the left of the entry hall, two steps down, a living room, dining room, billiard room, and oversize kitchen. To the right, a recreation room with wicker furniture, antique juke box, and television seating nest, and jutting out into the room a semicircular bar, paneled in split bamboo. Over the bar were hung crossed canoe paddles, with "Edgar" and "Lila" burned into their blades. The walls were hung with prints of famous golf holes. Behind the rec room, four large bedrooms, each with a bath.

Set off behind the kitchen was an ell that might have originally been a pantry but now held a set of gun cabinets and duck decoys. And tucked in behind that room, in what may have been the only addition since the house was built, a study. One of its walls was a stone fireplace; a second held books whose pages,

Spector guessed from the perfect leather crescents of their bindings, had never seen an inquiring face.

A passageway led to the double-door garages, three in all, and all filled with cars. Over the garages were musty suites originally used for help.

Be it ever so humble, he said aloud.

And so, when he came across the foodstuffs arranged as his mother might have done in the gray, two-story frame house she still lived in, the house he had been raised in, he recognized the pattern. A cultural totem. Where to keep the paper matches.

The telephone rang again. Again Parish's disembodied voice. This time the caller hung up.

Spector realized the exposure. Urso. Anthony Urso. He pulled the new recording machine from his suitcase. It took him several minutes to free it from its plastic wrap and polyurethane-foam blocks. All the while he imagined that Urso would call, wrecking the fragile glass of his construct. Finally he had it free. He replaced the telephone receiver from the old machine to the new. Then he slotted the cassette tape in the machine, tested it, and recorded his own greeting.

"Hello. You have reached the residence of Mr. and Mrs. Edgar Parish. No one can come to the phone. Please leave your message at the tone."

Callers who knew Parish's voice would not be undone by a stranger. More important, callers who knew him as Parish would hear the voice and be subliminally assured. The same unconscious assurance you get when you send an envelope to a name without a face and a person using that name turns up with your letter.

He saw the courier delivery truck weave down the driveway. A young man pulled his coat over his head and ran to the front door.

"Thanks," Spector called as he took the package.

"Sign here."

He was offered a clipboard and pen.

Instinctively, he began to write his given name. He saw its initial and caught himself, finishing off in an indecipherable scrawl.

"Got it," the fellow said. "Keep dry."

Spector waved as he drove off. Hadn't his mother always tipped delivery people? Where are the old virtues?

He opened the oversize envelope. Inside, a Chinese puzzle, a second sealed envelope, bearing the label of Empire State Bank. And inside that a short note from an obviously rushed Urso.

Dear Mr. Parish:
Here's a standard loan application. In addition we'll need from you (1) proper collateral, (2) a bank verification, and (3) most recent two years' tax returns, Form 1040 complete, but without schedules.
Hoping we can be of service to you.
Sincerely yours,
Anthony J. Urso
Ass't Vice-President

Spector set up shop at the large desk in the study. It was an excellent piece, a massive rosewood partner's desk. The top was inlaid with a rectangle of red leather, tooled with acanthus and vines. There were three frieze drawers across the top, three short drawers down the right pedestal, and on the left a cupboard. The plinths were made of a lighter wood, and he guessed they were oak.

He had brought along two yellow pads, and he set them out beside Urso's correspondence and the loan application. He studied the bank's communiqué carefully and noted down the unanswered questions:

1. Annual income
2. Financial statements
3. Tax returns
4. Property—legal description
5. Dependents
6. Employment—does EP work? did he ever?
7. SS number
8. Schedules for life ins., securities.

The answers must come from this house. He suppressed a rising wave of doubt and slowly opened the center drawer of Edgar Parish's desk.

The house was quiet. He heard only the rustling of his own movements as the drawer slid toward him. The compunction he felt about embezzlement was a rational one, born of a knowledge of crime and punishment. His reluctance about peering into another man's desk was rooted in deeper soil. If there were anything in the entire scheme for which he felt remorse, it was this.

The drawer contained none of the missing data. Stamps, clips, several snapshots, an address book. He removed the last for bedside reading. The drawers to either side held nothing of interest.

In the desk cupboard he found a decanter filled with a foul-smelling sherry, a kit for cleaning guns, and two ancient tins of pipe tobacco whose labels showed they had been mixed to order.

He tugged at the three pedestal drawers. They were locked. A single keyhole in the topmost drawer controlled them.

Spector returned to the left frieze drawer where he'd found the same stationery on which Parish had inquired of him. He drew out a sheet and, using a felt-tipped pen from the desk, printed a message to the Parishes' banker.

John Dixon:
Anthony Urso of Empire State Bank may call you about me. I'm doing some New York business and thought I ought to have a local bank. Please give him whatever he wants, copies of the trusts, the whole shebang. Lila and I will be traveling.

E.M.P.

That done, he stamped and addressed the envelope and placed it in his billfold for mailing. The Lake Forest postmark would add verisimilitude.

It was mid-afternoon Chicago time. No particular rush. Yet Spector knew that his plan was a race to cross the tracks before discovery. He had no deadline for his return to New York, but the fewer days spent as, alternatively, Roger Weedman and Edgar Parish, the better.

As he closed the drawer, he had an irrational sense of dread. He knew, as if a hand had been placed on his shoulder, that he was being watched. And from no more than a few feet. The taste of nausea filled his mouth, faintly redolent of the air-line lunch. What am I doing? I'm looking for a pen. A pen, the felt-tipped one, lay on the pad in front of him. An eraser? A ruler?

And, as close as he feared, he heard a sound, a whisper. Undecided still on his explanation, he turned.

There, gazing at him diffidently, sat a large gray cat.

Spector recovered in a few seconds. His heart kept a sprinter's pace. He called to the cat in surrogate friendship, but the animal extended a rear leg and began to wash.

There are five in the house, she had said. I must remember things.

He arose and began a systematic search of the house. He began in the basement. People often store files of important but useless papers. That's where old tax returns would go. He knew, in his own case, that the accountant had the full set and that he was careless about maintaining duplicates. In the Parishes' basement he learned that his hosts collected butterflies, Meissen china, duck stamps, commemorative plates, Tiffany Christmas decorations, and matchbooks. They had towels, golf tees, and ashtrays from every famous resort he could think of. They anticipated a nuclear attack or the Apocalypse itself, and could survive for decades on a store of canned peaches and bottled water. But no tax returns.

There was no attic. He moved to the master bedroom. He searched with apprehension, hoping that he would not stumble upon a secret collection of necrophilia or the unguents and ointments of an aging passion. He found three sets of golf clubs and, in Mr. Parish's closet, a floor safe too small to be the cache of his concerns. There were neither surprises nor papers.

Is it possible that this cannot be done? Is it possible that Parish has his bank prepare his returns, run his money, keep track of him? *Everyone* leaves a paper trail in this world. Perhaps, if you're wealthy enough, you can be followed by a sweeper. The possibility of failing when he had come so far only now occurred to Spector.

He made his way to the garage. There he found, in various recumbencies, the missing four cats. On a rainy afternoon, they were resting up for their own revels. Upstairs, in the servants' quarters, was a promising sight. Several cartons had been taped shut and stacked against the bookcases.

He slit the tape and began with the topmost box. Letters from their son, Edgar Jr., at military school, at camp, briefly and unsuccessfully at college. Photo albums. Several knit doilies, the product of a kindergarten craft hour.

Spector felt his spirits sink. This was a mad idea. There were only two boxes left.

In the penultimate one, he came close. There, stacked and packaged by year, were securities position statements for every year from 1960 to 1980. And they disclosed what Spector knew to be true: that the Parishes had a bundle socked away, that one or the other of them was the distributive beneficiary of large trusts, and that he could make a hell of a case for lending them money if he only had the facts.

But these statements were hopelessly outdated. The firm handling the trades, he remembered, had been gobbled up by one of the large insurance conglomerates five years ago. Maybe the last box.

He slit open its taping expectantly. Inside were cardboard folders, boxes in mock pebble design, with red tie ribbons. "Important Documents," read a script label.

He pulled a ribbon end and the bow gave. He removed a handful of important-looking papers entitled "Certificate."

And he read of the sire and dam of Lady Luck Linda, a Siamese, of James' Baby Blue, a Mangay. He had unearthed a storehouse of cat pedigrees.

Spector poured a generous portion of Irish whiskey into a lead-crystal glass. It was seven o'clock. He had hit on, amid the Johnny Mathis and Fred Waring, a tape of *Mozart's Greatest Hits*. The Parishes had probably neglected to send back the remittance card. He moved to the kitchen and began preparing a spaghetti sauce. He hadn't cooked since—when?—settling his capital account with the firm. One good meal on Edgar and Lila. The whiskey raised his spirits, and he decided to open a bottle of the '79 Margaux he had found in the cellar rack. And so, with the *Jupiter* filling the air and long Japanese mushrooms sizzling in butter, he reviewed his day.

Not a success. Destination seized, objective remains in enemy hands. Tomorrow he would do the other wing, the highboy in the living room, the chests, the upper kitchen cabinets, even the duck room.

The meal was excellent, the wine special. He was in bed, in

one of the guest bedrooms, dozing off, his disappointment dulled as his senses had been sated. And as the last slit of consciousness was closing, he thought of it. The study. The cat had interrupted him. The locked desk.

9

He sat up and turned on the lamp on the nightstand. It was just midnight. He strode down the hall to the master bedroom, then to Parish's closet—when he'd been through it earlier, he had noted its contents—and tugged from its hanger a white terry-cloth robe. "Mauna Lani" was stitched in blue over the breast pocket. He slipped it on and tied the belt. He went quickly through the house, flicking on the light switches as he moved.

In the far wing of the house the cats, who had in the darkness reclaimed their territory, scurried to cover. Once Spector settled down, they came out to observe.

He viewed the study. The ample desk. Beside it, he had not noticed before, a chest with four drawers. Same period—early Victorian. He spoke to it: Don't be locked.

It was.

Three drawers of the desk and four of the chest. And he without even a rudimentary knowledge of how to force a nineteenth-century lock. So much for the liberal arts.

He went to the kitchen and filled the coffee maker. Then he went about cadging his needs. From the breezeway, where most of the tools were stored, he took a cold chisel, a four-inch awl with a wooden ball handle, several lubricants, and a flashlight. Next stop, the master bedroom. In Mrs. Parish's dresser, under the lingerie, were two boxes. One held the jewelry Spector guessed she saved for daywear. Not of sufficient importance for the floor safe. Do women place their jewelry in the same spot for the convenience of thieves? he wondered. He knew the second box contained a miscellany of objects, and even his casual glance estimated them to be of sentimental rather than market value. If only one could convert the first to the second. Now, there's a good business concept. But of course several ventures had beaten him to the idea. Water from Lourdes and clods of earth from Graceland.

In among the buttons, medals, and foreign coins were keys. Some were labeled and were evidently superannuated: boat house, Packard, Annie's. But most were loose and unidentified. He carried the box with him, stopped in the kitchen to fill a large mug with coffee, and sat down at the desk.

Only four of the keys were of the skeleton variety, needed for this lock, and none worked. He shone the beam into the opening and poked the point of the awl around. How was it that every actor in every black-and-white mystery knew how to do this and not he? He could see nothing of interest, and if his tool hit a point of leverage, he did not know it.

Spector put off the decision as long as he could maintain interest in the tools. The value of the desk and its beauty dissuaded him from what he knew would be looked upon as wanton. He had no confidence he could pry the lock without destroying a piece of furniture made before Victoria was widowed. And though he had not forgotten that, in a list of his peccaries, the law would surely rank this one at the bottom, he found vandalism distasteful, vandalism of art indefensible.

What were the alternatives? Tomorrow was Monday. The library would be open. So would a hardware store, a locksmith. He might find a book to help him. He could certainly buy every skeleton key available. He could tell the locksmith that he had been house sitting and—what? He was at a dead end. Every fiction he could dream up was either dangerous or stupid.

Reluctantly he picked up the chisel, inserted its edge in a chamois to avoid scratching, and placed the scabbarded tip between the crosspiece and the top of the pedestal latch.

What force is needed to knock someone out? To open a rosewood desk? Spector's first taps were tenuous. He drew back and struck the heel of his hand to the chisel with what he imagined was a blow of the martial arts. A crack like the report of a deer rifle sounded. In its aftermath, Spector heard his heart, the cats scrambling, and an echo deep in the garages.

He looked down to see—he didn't know what. Blood? Hanging from the skin of its varnish was a two-inch slab. The lip of the drawer had broken clean, below the latch. Perhaps it could be mended.

He tugged on the brass pull of the middle drawer. He knew at once he was on to something. The desk had been modified— the philistines—to make a double drawer deep enough to hold modern files. And because the weight would encumber its opening, a modern system of rollers and slides had been installed in the cabinetry.

The drawer held a tablet-sized checkbook, and eight or ten manila files. He withdrew the contents and stacked them on the desk. Behind the papers were boxes of canceled checks, labeled by years, four briar pipes, a Colt automatic without clip, and several keys. He tried them in the shard of wood and indeed found one that worked. He rolled his chair to the chest and used a second key to open its single lock.

Satisfied, he went back to the folders. They contained conformed copies of the Parishes' wills and inter-vivos trusts. Goddamn, thought Spector. I hope you haven't given it away.

In the second folder were copies of older documents: trusts settled by their parents and grandparents. Spector read them quickly. He knew little about the field, but enough to realize it was free assets he had to find, not a beneficial interest. He spotted each of Lila and Edgar's names in separate documents. How nice for them. They each were income beneficiaries. Them that has shall get.

The next folders held a series of bank statements. Computer printouts. All from First Illinois. Dated, summarized, titled. They were the mother lode.

First were the trust accounts. Several million in each. Sensibly deployed between taxables and tax-frees, between debt and equities. Spector could see the committee meetings, the rehearsed sagacity, the endless economic justification that had been expended to get this far. He had no taste for money management. It occupied a cadre of people at his old firm, and they all seemed diligent people, people of good will. But to Spector it was a field of "Do miracles, show science," and the best of them acknowledged its element of sorcery. It was also an endeavor where, as the snide saying goes, if you were smart you ought to be rich. Most trust officers weren't rich.

The next three folders held, in order, the custodian-account statements for Edgar M. Parish, Lila R. Parish, and Edgar and Lila Parish as joint tenants.

Spector had not anticipated producing an impersonation of Lila. In order to part with her interests, he would need her signature, and so he put away everything but the statements for Edgar. They were ample for his purposes. They showed that Edgar owned, outright, almost three million dollars in traded securities.

Spector learned from the trusts that none had distributed its corpus and that Edgar would have to die before the body of assets was doled out. And Spector guessed from everything he had seen so far that Edgar had never worked a day in his life. How, then, does one accumulate $2.9 million in marketable securities, free and clear, his very own delectable nest egg? For a rainy day—not for living expenses, since the trust-income statements showed that Edgar's spending money came in from distributions at the rate of seven hundred thousand dollars a year.

Not, Spector knew, by saving lunch money. His parents would not have agreed, but the fact of it was that the Parishes, for all their economic clout, lived simply. No racehorses, cocaine, villas on the Costa del Sol. Their wealth, though it would seem to the common man to enable plutocratic excess, allowed the Parishes to pay taxes on their income (or, rather, on the half of it that was taxable), live comfortably, and play in the stock market. How many shotguns, how much single-malt whiskey, how many putters can one man buy?

Spector put a paper clip on the most recent statements and the ones from a year ago, and set them aside. He replaced the other folders in the drawer.

There were several other files. He still didn't have a financial statement or the tax returns. He was certain, however, they would be here.

He was wrong. One file contained matters about the house. Surveys, roofing bills, a plot plan of the gardens. A second held the deed and papers about a house in Wisconsin, on Lake Oconomowoc, owned in Lila's name and that of another woman—Spector guessed, her sister. And a third held similar documents for a house in Treasure Cay, Eleuthera. That was in Edgar's name. Spector made notes quickly: purchase price, debt at Dominion Bank of Nassau, property description. There were even rental records: it looked as if the Parishes used the beach house in January each year and rented it to friends for the Christmas and spring holidays.

The remaining files had no utility. Still, Spector read them with a growing sense of warmth for Edgar Parish. One contained memorabilia from 1952, when Edgar had apparently accompanied his father, a National Committeeman, as a delegate to the Republican convention. There were Taft buntings to be pinned to the lapel, ticket stubs, and a letter from his father bemoaning the "turn down the road of assimilation" that the convention had taken in nominating Dwight Eisenhower.

The last file was a series of letters addressed to Edgar at this very address, written in 1948 and 1949. One packet was from Lila, written when she was an undergraduate at Bradford Junior College. A second had no return address, but the hand was clearly a woman's and not Lila's. You old dog, Edgar. Spector put the letters back into the file and replaced it in the drawer.

He turned toward the unlocked chest. He was tired, and, although pieces of the puzzle were still missing, he was relieved to find that the drawers contained only heavy silver. This house would pose difficult problems of selection for a burglar.

He turned out the lights. It was two-thirty. Exhausted, exhilarated by the coffee and his find, Spector flopped on the Parishes' king-size bed and waited. And sleep came.

10

In the morning the rain had stopped. Spector stood in the kitchen, halving a honeydew melon and gutting its insides into the sink. Every window in the Parishes' house gave a lush prospect, and the one in front of him was particularly green and full. He looked out over the terraced steps to the Jacuzzi and the pool house beyond. A black chestnut tree stood between him and the morning sun, and light glistened off its wet, dark leaves. Too bad he would have to leave this house. He was beginning to enjoy it.

Promptly at seven-thirty Chicago time, eight-thirty New York, he called Urso. Not in yet. Exactly right. Spector left the Parishes' number. Then he sat down to the meal he had spread for himself, melon, eggs, sausage, muffin, and apricot conserve. Must remember to get in a few sets with Lauren this weekend. Method acting doesn't mean reaching Parish's dimensions.

He dressed in worsted slacks and a polo shirt, and tied a white cotton sweater around his neck. Anyone seeing him drive out of the property in the Parishes' Wagoneer would know that he was too at ease to be up to chicanery. He looked like one of their own children. One of them.

He found the small shopping center Lila had mentioned. In its corner, by a shoe-repair shop, was a freestanding pay phone. He had his bright-yellow can full of change, and he dumped a handful of quarters onto the shelf. Then, taking his own address book from his hip pocket, he started his calls.

It didn't take long. Five calls, three dates, starting mid-morning tomorrow. He had a dozen acquaintances on Wall Street who were peddling institutional-grade private placements. All three he had found in that morning were delighted to spend time with him tomorrow, to show him the prospectuses of deals they were pushing. Yes, they assured him. These would be perfect for a wealthy couple in their sixties. Make the investment, gift it to their grandchildren under the Uniform Gifts to Minors Act at a low tax basis. If it hits, they can come back in for lifetime enjoyment, or they can let their offspring take the gain at significantly lower rates. Sounds great. Come on by. We'll show you what we have.

The next call involved some delicacy. Several years ago Spector had worked on the sale of a closely held business—computer peripherals, if he remembered right—whose owner moved money abroad after the closing. Spector had seen lots of Swiss bank accounts, but this deal he thought far slicker. Under recent treaty amendments, most foreign accounts can be discovered by U.S. authorities if they can produce grounds for belief that a felony has occurred. Especially Switzerland. The Department of the Treasury had had a bellyfull of Switzerland.

Not so Panama.

Spector's client, whom he believed to be an honest but cautious man, had created a Panamanian trust prior to closing. The proceeds from sale went, if Spector recalled, first to a Mexico City bank and then to fund the offshore trust. He himself had not been involved in the creation of the channel, but he remembered the name of the man who had. A vice-president of Banco Nacional, main branch in the Zona Rosa. Now he stood in a suburban-Chicago shopping mall pleading in vacation Spanish with the secretary in Mexico City not to hang up but to find Señor Ramón Guitterez.

Contact was made. Spector used a fanciful name—taking it from the window of the shoe-repair store—but linked himself by using as a reference the name of the senior partner of his old firm. Simon Sebastian. Yes, Guitterez remembered what they had done for Mr. Sebastian. Yes, they had found the Panama lawyers and the Panama banks. Yes, he would be happy to do it again for Mr. Sebastian. It wasn't for him? He would be happy to do it for Mr. Sebastian's friend. They would get fee information and time requirements and call back. Certainly they could

66

leave the information on a recording machine, if the gentleman would just give him the number.

Money moves across borders in many ways. When the flow is regulated or prohibited, its transportation rises to a sub-art. You buy exportable products and sell the exports in bulk. You buy steel with Philippine pesos, on board in Hong Kong, and sell the steel that day to a Seattle construction firm. The money ends up in a U.S. account. If the buyer suspects you to be moving restricted currency, be prepared for a haircut, a deep haircut. On one memorable occasion, Spector had opened up simultaneous bank accounts in New York and Lusaka, Zambia, both in the name of the Society of Jesus. A significant sum, well into seven figures, moved mysteriously and intact from the African nation, which prohibited withdrawing more than the equivalent of a thousand dollars, to an account at Forty-fifth Street and Park Avenue.

But those were all traceable transactions. Unless Guitterez remembered the voice of the young associate who had assisted Sebastian on the peripherals company, here he had left no footsteps. From Guitterez' comments about the fee structure, he seemed less interested in the source of this business than in its potential for contribution. Nothing regional about that.

Spector raked the shelf below the telephone to gather his unspent quarters. When he turned around, he faced an attractive, tanned woman, chestnut, short-cropped hair, mid-forties. She had a faint scolding look on her lips, and her eyes smiled at him.

"Did it come up three plums?"

"Excuse me?"

"The telephone. You look as if you're a winner."

"Oh." He shook the tennis-ball can self-consciously. Had she heard his conversation? Spector was trying to recall whether his side alone would have been damaging.

"You're Lila Parish's young man."

"Yes, I am. How did you know?"

"You have their car." She didn't look away. He did, to see if the Wagoneer was where he had parked it.

"I'm right next door. I saw your lights come on last night and thought you might be running around in the nude. We don't get much beefcake in Lake Forest."

"I didn't know you could see me," he said.

67

He thought her brow raised at the corner, but if so it was for the briefest moment. "I couldn't. But from that blush I wish I had."

Spector was knocked off balance and he didn't enjoy the position. But she wasn't ready to let him recover. She had Wedgwood-blue eyes and a taut figure covered in a cream blouse with a blue monogram and linen skirt. A brown herringbone. He wanted to look more closely but demurred as she held his eyes with hers.

"I'm Carol Kittredge."

"Hello."

"Hello. Do you have a name?"

"Oh, yes." Spector was faltering. He had several.

"Would you consider me too forward if I wanted to . . ." She paused suggestively. He didn't know what to expect. ". . . use it."

"Ma'am?"

"Use it. Your name."

"Oh, no. It's Weedman. Roger Weedman."

She seemed satisfied. She reached in a straw clutch purse and took out a pair of sunglasses. She looked at him once more with unshaded eyes and put them on. The act had an inexplicable intimacy, as if she were dressing.

"Since we're neighbors, Roger, with the Parishes away, you drop by if"—and she paused, though he could not tell why—"you want to borrow a cup of gin."

Jesus, he thought. Great work, Spector. Chastity defended by stupidity.

Would a dalliance interfere with his work? At first he had imagined that being single again would be a sexual smorgasbord. In fact, since he had left Joan or she him, he had as little interest in his libido as in the stock market. And after embarking on his new career, he simply hadn't thought about it. Odd, he said aloud, as he watched the linen-wrapped haunch of Carol Kittredge cross the parking lot. She had a practiced walk, one that had been watched before.

He came up with no answer to his question. Instead he ran his last chores. He shopped for some one-pot meals. The elaborate sauce of last night was an indulgence. Then a trip to the IRS office at Northwestern Station to pick up a Form 1040 for the last two years. The individual return.

"You pretty late," the black woman behind the counter said.

"C'mon, sister," he said. "Uncle Sam hasn't missed it. You *know* he's got too much and you and I don't have enough."

She laughed and shook her head.

Back home in Lake Forest. Urso, bless his emulous soul, had called. His voice on the machine was earnest and self-conscious.

Spector got him back.

"It all looks in order, Mr. Urso. I should be dropping off a completed application with you Wednesday."

"Well, you certainly work fast. Now, tell me, Mr. Parish, what will the size of this credit be, and what's its purpose?"

"I have in mind a line in the low seven figures. That range, Mr. Urso. Fully covered, of course, by big-board securities. And as for the purpose, I'd guess you'll want to call it money to go play in the traffic."

That deliberately incautious phrase was used in the business for investment loans to wealthy individuals. Spector liked the casting of Edgar Parish as hip, just short of glib.

"I'll bring the prospectus for the deal I'm looking at, but I assume, what with the rules of the Fed, you won't want to use it for collateral."

"No, that's right," said Urso. The Federal Reserve Board prohibits banks from lending against securities purchased with the proceeds of the loan. Urso sounded impressed that his customer knew it.

"You'll be in Wednesday, then?"

"I'll be here. We'll look forward to seeing you. I've already assigned this loan to one of our best young officers. We'll look forward to meeting you."

The final call of the series was to United for reservations on Tuesday's early flight into LaGuardia. He could check into a hotel and be downtown by ten.

Spector had had a productive day. Cramped by the thought of the trip, he changed into shorts, a tee shirt, and sneakers. Outside, the freshly washed foliage of the Parishes gave off a deep woody scent. The sun sat low, enlarged and red in the summer haze. Its refracted light hung over the suburb. He ran easily down Parmalee to the county road, then at a steady pace jogged several side roads to their end. After half an hour he turned for home. Once there, he flicked on the one Mozart tape, and turned the machine up to the highest volume so the sound rattled through the empty house. He drew a bath in the sunken tub adjoining the master bedroom, and fixed a small pitcher of martinis to accompany himself.

Afterward a simple supper out of a can, with a split of Beychevelle. Am I fitting into Edgar Parish's skin a bit too readily? Given a few years, a few pounds, could I be he? As he turned out the house lights for bed, he peered into the darkness to where he imagined the Kittredge house was. He could see nothing.

11

In the solitude of the plane ride Spector sat quietly and drafted the financial statement of Edgar and Lila Parish. It was reportorial fiction, a creation of fancy that needed only a few facts as its foundation. He prepared a joint disclosure, because the numbers were impressive and because it again confirmed the obvious: that the man who had control of this much detail could only be Edgar Parish.

He examined his handiwork with a critical eye. Impressive, whether produced by inheritance or imagination. Since he had found no mortgage payment in the checkbook, Spector listed the Lake Forest house as free and clear. And he had fixed its market value by calling ads in the Sunday real-estate listings. For the Wisconsin and Caribbean properties, he guessed at market values. No bank would be inclined to challenge those, though he was mindful to keep the Eleuthera house value in proper proportion to its mortgage. He excluded any remainder interests in the trusts. Might as well be conservative. There would be plenty for his purposes without bragging. In sum, he showed the Parishes, thus endowed, to be worth a bit over eight million dollars.

A little less than half of that was Edgar's, outright. For income, he had several hundred thousand a year in his own name from the trusts, more than ample to service the loan Spector had planned for him. Spector looked at the one remaining blank line on the loan application: Occupation. His diligence had revealed none for Edgar Parish, past or present. He had checked the Lake Forest and Chicago business telephone directories, Parish's personal address book, and Parish's entry in the various club directories he had found around the house. Spector took his fountain pen and completed the application with one word: "Investments."

The tax return was more difficult. Spector had few guidelines. By the same token, he knew that, unlike the financial statement, it would not be corroborated. A credible attempt would pass muster.

Investment income was easy. He had the custodian reports. He added some rental income from Eleuthera, excluded the Wisconsin house as Lila's, decided on a fashionable amount of oil-and-gas royalties, and called it quits. The deduction and credit entries of the return were more difficult. Clearly, even though he had not been able to find any, taxpayers in these stratospheric heights would have elaborate shelters. Not simply positions in municipal bonds. Spector invented a few, ran a depreciation schedule through his Hewlett-Packard calculator to come up with Edgar's present value, and listed the total on the fictive return.

For the other entries—charitable giving, interest expense, state taxes—the Treasury Department happily prints summaries of past years' average returns. The ratios are inapposite to taxpayers in the Parishes' range. Still, the numbers allowed Spector to come up with believable guesses. When it came to deductions, Spector had to improvise on his own. A cappella. Their checkbooks showed few charities. But Spector wanted the Parishes to show to advantage, and since he didn't need to fund the donations he created, he gave lavishly to the Chicago Symphony, the Boy Scouts, and Community Chest.

He needed a signature for the return in a writing other than his own. He decided to clip the preparation stamp from his own returns, and paste it to the Parishes' before making copies for the bank. That would allow the authorities to trace, but he used a large, national accounting firm. They must prepare several hundred thousand returns a year. He would drop these drafts off at a secretarial service today, and have plenty of time for cutting and pasting.

The plane landed and taxied to its gate. Everyone stood, waiting the longest wait. He was eager to go. In the crammed aisle in front of him, teenagers on a high school class outing shouted back and forth excitedly. Several were wearing head-phones attached to portable cassette players. Two boys in front of Spector got out their passports and compared photos.

He had to have one. He couldn't keep his funds in the U.S., given the lengthy reporting requirements of domestic banks. No, the money would have to travel until it could be brought back clean. And if he was stuck in the country, offshore funds would be a liability. There would be wire transfers to a local bank, the need for taxpayer indentification numbers, regular inquiries by the Internal Revenue Service. Foreign bank accounts for U.S. taxpayers had been under scrutiny ever since Bernie Kornfield and Robert Vesco had parked their fortunes abroad. Too bad, thought Spector. Ninety-five percent of the bad apples give the rest of us a bad name.

He had one more possibility. He left the plane and walked through the sterile corridors toward the baggage pickup. He stopped by a row of telephones, opened Edgar Parish's battered, belted leather briefcase, and found his own address book.

She was an old girlfriend. Before Joan. After his divorce he had sought her out and she had been, as he remembered, pliant, comforting, and dull. Sonya Penner. I'm the perfect exit lady, aren't I? she had said. You exit from the emotional involvement with your former wife, and I make no demands. Like a shower after tennis. She said it wistfully, but without self-pity.

Sonya was the head of art for an ad agency. She saved her animus, she used to say, for the office. What she wanted from a man was no hassle. She had gone to bed with him as casually as she might brush her teeth, and with the same indifference.

Sure, she told him. She'd love to see him. Tonight? Short notice, after—how long has it been—six months?—but she wouldn't stand on ceremony.

From the airport, his cab dropped him off at the New York Hilton. There he checked in as Edgar Parish and gave the bellboy an extra dollar to take the bag up to the room without him. A more modest hotel this time for the Parishes. For one thing, Edgar Parish was known at the Pierre. For another, Spector was beginning to worry about the sunk costs. He had thought his bankroll more than ample to get him through to the actual loan closing, but he might need it all for the false passport. The room at the Hilton was half the price of one at the Pierre. He changed, caught a cab hailed by the doorman, and raced downtown.

Now dressed in a uniform from old campaigns, a tailored gray suit with a chalk-white pencil stripe, slight tuck at the waist, suspenders in regimental colors, silk foulard tie, white shirt with English spread collar, he re-entered the halls of his past life. All three colleagues saw him promptly. He was now a potential buyer, and when you're a seller, no one is more important.

Their methods of operation were remarkably similar. Each had reserved a small conference room, each offered coffee served in good china, and each had typeset and spiral-bound memoranda to show him. Quizzed on the nature of his agency, Spector declined to give specific information. Instead he let on that he was doing some work "in an unstructured way" for a significant but publicity-shy family of American industry. He was looking for some sound investments. Tax shelter was a consideration, but not the driving one. The deal he was at present looking for was in the one-to-two-million range. No start-ups, no high-risk mezzanines. They should have some asset base, the kind of thing that would pass muster if shown to the family banker, and should be in all respects toward the established side of the venture spectrum.

Each of the three nodded judiciously as Spector talked. Each of the three thought he might have just what Spector was looking for. Spector took a memorandum from each of them, placed at his request in a manila envelope, and signed a receipt including a statement that he or his principal was an accredited investor. After the last meeting, he declined lunch and hailed a cab bound uptown. He had left an address or phone number with none of them.

He stopped at his apartment, thumbed through the mail, all "occupant" stuff, and tossed it in the zinc garbage pail by the front steps. Upstairs he pulled together some clean clothes. One last cab, back to the Hilton as Edgar Parish. It took minutes to prepare the tax returns for copying. He looked quickly at the three memoranda. Any of them would do. They were professional, and they would impress a young bank officer with their gravity, their seriousness of purpose. Invested capital was a serious matter.

One was particularly suitable. A successful chain of restaurants was raising several million dollars privately on a sale-and-lease-back program. Thirty individual units were offered, at $170,000 each. There was real estate behind the investment, giving it the kind of conservative patina he needed, but it wasn't the kind of deal a bank would lend on directly. If the restaurant chain went under, the buildings had no other purpose, and the bank would have to look elsewhere to get its loan repaid. He threw the other two memoranda in the wastebasket under his Formica desk. Then he called the three brokers and told them he had chosen a different deal, but thanks anyway. They urged him to keep in touch, and he promised he would.

He was now prepared. Tomorrow the bank itself. With any luck, one of only two appearances, the first to ask for the money, the second to pick it up. What would he do in the meantime? He checked his list. Ah, yes. The passport. Perhaps he could cross that off after his date tonight. Sonya would help. She had never refused him anything.

He called the Parishes' number. The recording machine answered, and with his transmitter he triggered the replay mechanism. Urso again: he had been in touch with Mr. Dixon at First Illinois and he wanted to confirm the appointment for Wednesday. Two invitations to dinner for the Parishes. He noted those before erasing the tape. He would have to remember to leave a message. No word from Mexico.

He stripped to his underwear and lay on the freshly made bed. He had the Sunday *Times Magazine* section, and he flipped through its articles on the concerns and appetites of the rest of the world until he found the puzzle.

Would his parents be amused? he wondered. Putting aside the social consequences—they would be horrified at those. But on

74

a broader level. Would they appreciate the architectonics of the idea? Would they admire its sharpened ironies? Like most people who didn't have enough of it, his parents treated money in earnest. It was not a subject to amuse. They were certain that for everyone without wealth it was an instrument to change the world, and for everyone with it an instrument of stasis.

At the very least, his father would understand the appeal of this plan for Spector. If you meant to stand apart, to be distinct, nothing could beat ignoring the rules.

The evening with Sonya was pleasant. She was a fan of the dance, and he remembered and took her to a performance of the City Ballet. Afterward they had supper. They talked about people they used to know, about her career, which was flourishing, about Palestinian resettlement and Michael J. Fox. They did not discuss what he was doing, where he was living, and what he was feeling.

In the cab to her place he spoke up.

"Sonya, let me ask you a favor."

"Yes," she said flatly. "You can spend the night."

"That's not a favor. That's a jackpot." She smiled at his weak compliment. "No. A real favor. Your art department . . ."

"Yes?"

Spector could hear her surprise. He had always shown a faint deprecation of her business.

"They can do most anything, can't they? In terms of coming up with mock publications."

"What do you mean?"

"Well, remember that magazine you showed me? The one they had done for Time Inc., lampooning *People* magazine?"

"Yes. For the anniversary dinner."

"Well, you could do that for almost anything made of paper, couldn't you?"

"Do you want to tell me what you have in mind?"

He took a deep breath. Until then he had thought that a stage gesture.

"I have a client. He needs a passport. A fake one. In any name you like. He'll supply the picture. He'll pay."

"Are you nuts?"

"Can you do it?"

"Sure. At least I think so."

"Will you? You could do it at night. No one need know."

"You *are* nuts. First of all, I couldn't do it. It would take the entire department. Second, you couldn't keep it quiet. Third, it's illegal. I do not fancy my ass rotting away in some federal penitentiary. It's not considered good, career-wise."

"No?"

"No." The cab pulled up in front of her building. Her doorman opened the door.

Spector told the cab to wait. He got out and walked with her into the lobby.

"Sonya, it's late."

"Sure, Spector, sure. Look, it's not my business, but you're fooling around with dynamite. I know the market's in a slump, but it'll come back. Be careful, will you?"

"Yeah, sure." He was abstracted. He kissed her cheek and saw the elevator doors close around her.

12

What has become of the world of finance? Spector stood outside the main midtown office of Empire State. It has gone to hell. Not a post and lintel to be seen, no Romanesque masonry, not a single frieze depicting the history of commerce. No wonder bank stocks are down.

The façade of Empire State could have been that of an insurance company or a travel agency. Plate-glass windows wrapped around the first floor, allowing views of desks and the people at work behind them.

He had intended his early arrival, but the time he had allotted to pull himself together was now having quite the opposite effect. He remembered fondly the practical theatre course he had taken in college. The study of the art, the bloodless study, was easy. Not until a performance, minutes before, did he realize the hazards of climbing into another's character: the dizzy height, the narrow ledge, the nakedness of standing without the guide of history.

Again he stood before the curtain went up, his confidence melting. What can go wrong? What's the worst that can happen? Before today, when he imagined today, he could answer and remedy, until he could think of nothing else. He had plugged the holes that could be plugged. He knew what would go right: the collateral package, the financial statement, the tax return, his appearance. Where were the risks?

John Dixon. Dixon knew the Parishes, and in a conversation with Empire could let slip any one of the hundred things that would catch Spector up. The difference in age, most likely. Or that Edgar Parish had a drinker's nose, or thinning blond hair, or a way of talking that sprayed the listener. Spector felt he had dissuaded Urso from long talks with Dixon, but maybe more needed to be done. What else? The tax return was believable, but it was doubtless inaccurate. There were other investments Spector couldn't know of, probably several other shelters too. How would they be discovered? What if Edgar had several other bank accounts, and Spector had missed the primary one? What if a spot check with First Illinois showed not several thousand in cash but several hundred thousand? Could Parish be so cavalier, so indifferent to his money? Would Empire look upon a gross understatement of financial condition as they would a gross overstatement?

And there was the business of the Social Security number. Spector had the Parishes' actual numbers: they were printed in the checkbook. But to a knowing eye they disclose area and approximate date of birth. Spector had to choose between altering the number to show a younger man or running the risk, albeit slight, of getting a loan officer transplanted from Chicago. He chose the former, hoping that no one would notice.

Those were the answers he came up with. They were the

same answers he'd been getting for a week. Standing at Fifty-fourth Street and Park Avenue, conspicuous in his new clothes, Spector felt resolve seeping out of his pores. He shuddered from the imagined wetness, crossed the street, and entered the bank.

The lady at the information desk sent him to the elevators. Loans were on the third floor. Before Spector could ask, a pretty, dark-haired girl at the reception desk told him Mr. Urso was on his way. Was he imagining it or did she smile slightly at his dress? He had no time to worry about it. Suddenly someone was in front of him, pumping his hand. Tony Urso introduced himself.

Spector was not tall—maybe five feet ten. But he looked noticeably down into Urso's open face. He saw a man, his age, with soft, deep-set eyes that gave him a sleepless look. Perhaps to compensate, Urso smiled broadly, showing perfect teeth. He was a pudgy man, with a heavy beard. He wore a dark-blue poplin suit, and Spector could see the bulges in the arms where his sleeves had bunched in his rush to get to the elevator. Urso gave the impression that he was not yet familiar with working in a coat and tie.

And Urso saw his new customer. Not what he had expected by the phone voice. For one thing, younger. And no trace of the excesses that he liked to think go with a life of leisure. No, instead of the flabby rich kid he expected, he saw a man of average height and athletic build. True, from the tan you could tell the guy didn't work for a living and probably never had. Edgar Parish carried an old leather briefcase, so old you'd be embarrassed about it if you were a salaried employee, with "EMP" stamped in gold by the handles. A good-looking man, dark hair that came down to a sharp widow's peak. And he dressed—who else could get away with this but the rich?—as if he was on the pro golfers' tour. Gray flannel slacks, loafers with tassels, white patent-leather belt, white knit shirt, and sports jacket the color of the twist in a martini.

Urso led him through the corridors and peppered him with questions. His trip, the duration of his stay in New York, his hotel.

"I couldn't get into the Pierre this trip. They're filled. So I'm at the Hilton. On Sixth. It's a zoo."

"Gee," Urso said. He was sympathetic with the plight. "You'd think the Pierre would make space for you, being a good customer and all, Mr. Parish."

"One certainly would. But they've gone co-op, you know, with many of their units, so they don't have nearly the number of rooms they used to."

"Right," confirmed Urso. He was not going to be caught in what is the only sin of that island culture: being out of the know.

They entered a windowless conference room. Ten chairs around a laminate table. On the wall two Buffet prints. Urso asked the secretary stationed by the door to call a third person; Spector didn't catch the name.

"Incidentally, Tony," he said. "Since we're the same age and since I'm going to owe you money, why don't we go with first names?"

Urso beamed. "Absolutely. You're right."

"Mine's Ed. Not Edgar."

"Right, Ed."

"Can't stand 'Edgar.' Never could," Spector added truthfully.

The door opened, and through it walked a woman of startling beauty.

"Ed Parish. Meet Cynthia Olive. She'll be your loan officer."

Spector didn't realize his name had been called.

She was bemused by his open gaze. "Hello," she said.

She was his height, a touch taller. Like him she had dark hair and eyes, but her hair was black as a Bengali's and her eyes seemed to be cabochons of an impossibly soft mineral. Her brows went straight across her face. She wore a summer suit, houndstooth check, without a blouse. Around her neck was a slight gold chain, curving at its nadir over the bumps of her prominent collarbone.

"Hello," she said again.

"Hello," he answered. What insecurity he had had about his impersonation he now forgot and concentrated instead on how to impress this woman. It gave him a conviction not merely to be Edgar Parish, but to improve the character.

Urso outlined the process their loan committee would use. They had sent Ed the necessary papers. Had he received them? All that would have to be completed before the loan could be considered. Then the loan officer would make a recommendation to the committee and the usual inquiry would be done. If everything was in order, the committee would take up the recommendation at its weekly meeting and make a decision. If the decision was favorable, the loan could close shortly thereafter. The lawyers wanted him to say that he should not construe anything that was said or given to him as approval of the loan until the closing actually occurred, and that he should not do anything in reliance of his getting the loan until then.

It was a speech Spector could have given. He used the opportunity to gain furtive knowledge about Cynthia Olive. From the tabletop up, it was all positive.

She was aware of his examination and did nothing to arrest it. Careful, he thought. The main idea is to get a sizable chunk of money.

At an appropriate break in Urso's speech, Spector reached down and opened his briefcase. The few papers inside did not justify the size of the case—Edgar had several in his closet—but Spector liked the monogram and its aristocratic shabbiness. He took out his writings, palmed them into a neat pile, and looked to Cynthia in complicity.

She returned his glance coolly. "We want to hear from you, Mr. Parish. About the size of this credit line. Why you want it."

Spector nodded. I'll bet you do.

"What Tony says sounds fine to me. Understand, I'm not a businessman. I only use banks when I want to make an investment and not move money around. Right now I don't want to get out of the market. You'll appreciate why, I think. But my accountants tell me I need more shelter, I've got municipals up the wazoo, and I want to get tax relief without giving up the equity play.

"So I'm going to buy into a sale-and-lease-back deal White-Foreman is syndicating. My lawyers have checked it out, and they're satisfied with it. Here's the prospectus. You'll want to look at it."

He handed her the document he'd saved from yesterday's visits to Wall Street. It was an inch thick.

"Not quite a Triple A tenant, and some risk, I suppose, that you get the buildings back if they don't sell enough french fries. But good shelter, and real upside on the percentage lease.

"Now, I understand you can't lend so that I make this investment directly, and you wouldn't be satisfied with this as collateral. For my part, I don't want to pay for your lawyers to read the prospectus and understand it. I'm willing to pay usual closing costs for this loan, including laywers' fees, but not for that.

"So I'm proposing instead that you take as security my trading account at First Illinois. I'm going to buy ten units of this sale-lease-back—at one-seventy per that's a million seven—and my stocks in that account are worth almost double. I feel that's more than adequate collateral, and you may be surprised I'm giving up so much. But Lila and I travel a good deal and I don't want the bother of calls from the bank. They're like margin calls. Besides, I won't be doing anything else with these stocks, so you might as well have them. I want you to take that into consideration when you set the rate and fees on this loan."

"What term did you have in mind?" she asked.

"Write it up for a year. I'll pay ten or twenty percent down then and roll over the rest. If you don't like what you see when it's due, you call it and I'll pay it off."

"And the rate? You had some idea of the rate?" Spector wasn't entirely sure that she wasn't toying with him, drawing him out for the benefit of law-enforcement agents crouching at the keyhole.

"I'm a good credit, Miss Olive. I know that. I'm a rich man. I also know that every bank has customers who borrow below prime, and I have no doubt you find a way to make money on them. I'll settle for prime. Prime rate, no points."

The bankers were impressed. Cynthia Olive was the more reserved of the two, and her tone of voice was intended to convey the bank's objectivity.

"The rate, as you may know, Mr. Parish, is set by a committee only after it's decided to make the loan. That step is a long way off. We will have to look at the completed application, the returns. . . ."

As she spoke, Spector handed across the table each of the documents she named.

"You've thought of everything."

"I try not to waste time. And Tony here has been a great help." Make her understand you're not in this alone.

She leafed haphazardly through the papers while Urso looked on. Spector knew they were looking for a quick read of certain lines: Adjusted gross income. Net worth. Dealers in the great jade houses of the Orient are said to watch a customer's eyes for the dilation of the pupils, a sign of the autonomous nervous system that can't be controlled and that signals pleasure, the desire to buy. Urso squirmed in his chair. The large and ebon eyes of Cynthia Olive showed nothing.

"It's all here," she said.

Spector smiled. There were two possible readings of that line. He elected the plain meaning.

"I try to please."

She met his eyes. "I bet you do," she said softly.

"Now, I'm in no hurry, but White-Foreman is. And my guess is that, if your bank doesn't want this, the second bank I try will. So what I need from you is a prompt decision. If it's no, no big deal. But you have to tell me soon."

"We should be able to get this to committee in a week. Next Wednesday. We could close right after that."

"If approved," Olive said.

"Of course," Urso added with a shrug.

"And the only thing I ask is that, if you want to call anyone on this, especially John Dixon, you let me know in advance. He's awfully sensitive about my going elsewhere."

"Right," said Urso. They exchanged a fraternal look.

Cynthia Olive would not be excluded.

"We don't mean to say this is a done deal, you understand. We also like to have loan agreements, promissory notes, the usual banker's petty pleasures."

"Oh, I understand," Spector said. How could he warm her up? He sensed she didn't like this rich Chicagoan who knew too much about her business. "I'll sign away my life."

"Will your wife be signing?"

He had to look down to see what Cynthia meant. She was pointing to Lila's name on the tax return. Was that it? She had caught him flirting while Lila languished at home, knocking down vodka stingers at the Onwentsia Club?

"No," he answered. "She won't be signing. We do a lot of things separately."

He saw her eyes glint in recognition.

"I'll sign. And if I don't pay on time, you'll have me on your hip."

"I beg your pardon."

"On your hip. *Merchant of Venice*. It's a wrestling term, I think. It means the bank will be able to throw me for a fall."

"Oh," said Cynthia. "I thought it sounded like fun."

Urso stood up. Whether he felt the meeting had ended or had become too personal, Spector could not tell. But the timing was good. The meeting had gone well.

They both walked him to the elevator—on either side, like arresting officers. Spector wished Urso would go away. Remember, it's the money you came for. Don't let that libido swell and occupy the space reserved for the brain. It's happened before.

"I'm sure you won't find our form note and security agreements anything to worry about," Urso was saying. "They're really boiler-plate. But we have to have them. Banks like to lend money out and they like to get it back."

"I'm sure I'll find them fine. You have to protect yourselves too. Keep on your toes." Spector hoped she wouldn't take him up on the stupidity of his words.

"That's right," said Cynthia. She was so near he could smell her perfume, and her body under that scent. "You know what they say."

"What do they say?" His elevator was here and he didn't want to leave. She waited to answer until he was inside. The doors were closing.

"You snooze, you lose," she said.

13

Once his taxi broke through the wall at Fifty-seventh, they ran with light traffic. It was midday, and if ever you had to race to Kennedy for a plane, noon on a summer's day was the time to try it. Too bad I'm not in a rush.

I could really use more time to think, he realized as they hit the Triborough. I don't know what the hell I'm doing.

The meeting at the bank had elated him and filled him with a certitude that this deal could be done. The grand slam would include Cynthia Olive. Even without her, it could be done. He needed only a passport and the money. The money was out of his hands. But the other, he could take control of. Seeing those passports passed around loosely by the kids on the plane had made him realize it. *Carpe diem. Carpe documenta.*

Before he got out of the cab, he took off his jacket, folded it neatly in quarters, and put it carefully into the spacious briefcase. The international terminal was packed. Perhaps too crowded. European vacations coming to an end. He stood for a moment at a glassed-in balcony, watching the customs stalls below. Line upon line of suitcases, filled with the detritus of the summer: alpenstock hats, wood carvings, Florentine wallets, Harrod's preserves. They had moved dollars abroad. He was merely after the same effect without a change in ownership.

He went to the sundries counter and bought a can of shaving cream, a souvenir linen towel with the Statue of Liberty, and a razor.

Then he visited the men's rooms. Too large, too crowded, too close to security. He finally decided on his site: three stalls, three urinals, near enough to the gates to assure patronage among the incontinent. Though it was empty for the moment. Inside, the janitor's closet was open. He stored his briefcase and removed a zinc pail. He placed the pail, upside down, by the farthest stall, removed his shirt, placed the towel and razor on the sink, and waited.

The moment eluded him. People came and went, as he acted out half a dozen shaves. After the first he removed the blade. Only a few patrons went into the stalls. When they did, something else would go wrong. Either they wore no coats or the room had others at the sinks or urinals.

Half an hour went by. The shaving cream was running out, and he didn't want to face the odd look of the proprietor when he returned for a second can. Two men in suits walked in. They entered the stalls. He thought he saw, in the mirror, the top of a passport in the inside pocket of the one.

He moved quickly. He washed the soap from his face and dried off. He put on his shirt, retrieved his briefcase from the closet, and placed it by the sink, and waited seconds for the sounds from the stall to indicate a certain indisposition of its occupant. Then he boldly stepped on the pail and, reaching over, grabbed the coat from the hook and pulled.

"Hey. My coat. You fucker . . ."

In a single motion he emptied the inside pockets and let the comb, wallet, airline ticket sprawl to the floor. A blue document the size of a passport he stuck in his pocket. He grabbed his briefcase and ran. He was aware of the stall door swinging open, and an enraged man limping out, crouching like an early primate as he tugged his trousers from around his ankles.

In the corridor, Spector quickly opened his briefcase and put on the yellow jacket. He fell in among a family heading not, as a thief would be, toward the exit, but toward the airline portals.

He stopped at the security gates. Tens of others were lined up to see their arriving friends. He waited five minutes, more expectant than any of the others, not daring to look back. Once he thought he sensed a cadre of airport guards busying about behind him, but he craned forward for an imagined rendezvous and he didn't see them again. All the while, he had a nagging feeling that something was wrong with his hoist, that the passport hadn't looked right. Could he have stolen someone's trading-stamp book? Who would leave a perfectly comfortable stool for a down payment on matched luggage?

A short, swarthy man with broken English had elbowed through the crowd and was hustling his business to the incoming passengers.

"Limousine? Limousine to Manhattan. Forty bucks."

He was getting no takers. Spector grabbed him by the elbow.

"Doesn't seem as if my man is going to show. How much to midtown?"

The driver regarded him. Couldn't decide if he was a New Yorker or not. Seemed to be, but not in those clothes.

"Midtown, downtown. Same price."

"Too much."

"Thirty-five."

"Okay. Let's go."

"Tolls extra." Everybody has his own tug of war. The driver didn't want to leave any room on the plateau.

"Tolls extra," agreed Spector impatiently. He handed the driver his satchel and spun him around toward the exit.

They left the terminal without incident. He waited until the limo was clear of the airport throughway and was speeding along the Van Wyck. Only when they had hit sixty did he feel unwatched. Then, furtively, he slid out the small book he had stuck into his pants pocket. It was the right color. But he realized what was wrong. It was too small.

Canadian.

He had lifted a damned Canadian passport. Too late now. No exchanges, no refunds. Cyrus MacNeil Feade, 1470 Witherspoon, Toronto. Occupation: Sales. Five foot eight, 160 pounds. So far so good. Hair brown, eyes hazel. No good— Spector was batting five hundred. Never mind. It would have to do. Has there ever been a border policeman who looked deeply into your eyes? The face of Cyrus MacNeil Feade looked back at him openly, even a little startled. He couldn't place it on that dwarfed figure charging from the toilet stall like a rodeo bull. Sorry, Cy, he said aloud. No offense.

"You want no fence?" the driver asked, surprised.

"No," said Spector. "Just mumbling. Make believe I never said a word."

14

He checked out of the Hilton and, yellow coat stashed in the one-suiter, walked the two miles to his apartment. No sense incurring needless costs. And there was plenty to do in New York. He knew from popular fiction that computers could re-create the calls made to and from a touchtone phone. He stopped on Columbus Avenue at a public booth, called the Parishes' house, and with his pocket transmitter operated the recording machine. No messages.

Back to his own apartment. Spector felt as if he were intruding on another's life, not coming home. There were the sparsely stocked cabinets, the empty refrigerator, the mail from no one he knew. It had been fun being Edgar Parish. Parish was a man with a soil around him, a soil rich in nutrients of family, club, even the damn duck decoys. You had to hand it to Edgar. He didn't fret about the lack of purpose to his purposeless life.

Spector had a full agenda. The new passport would need a new photo and, he had decided, a new name. Once he figured out how to do that, he had to pad the name with life. Like papiermâché. A new post-office box, new credit cards, library cards all in the created identity. This time it was easy. Spector knew which buttons worked and which didn't. Down to Twelfth and Broadway, to the Strand, his favorite used-book store. He bought an old history, *This Nation Called Canada*. On the way uptown, a stop at the Forty-second Street newsstand for back issues of the Toronto *Globe and Mail*.

Thursday and most of Friday he did his reading. He wrote out checks and envelopes for Lauren, organized them by month into six packets. He wrapped each packet in a wide rubber band and labeled each by month with a yellow sticker. Then he canceled his cleaning lady. Mostly she had put empty soup cans in the garbage sack and put the garbage sack in the incinerator. For forty bucks a week. Leaving no tracks seems to come naturally to me.

Friday afternoon he called Lauren at work to make sure their game was still on.

"Hey, I remember. Why you checking up?"

"No reason," said Spector. "Labor Day and all. I just wanted to make sure."

In fact, he was tiring of the solitude, and he knew he faced more, a long stretch. This was human contact. Or as close as he got these days. Once removed. More and more often, there was something in between. He dealt with people through artifacts. A dollar bill, a tennis ball. We hand the usher a ticket, he hands us a stub. When do we touch?

Cynthia Olive came to mind, and the thought stirred in his groin. It's been a long time. What the hell have I been about? How did I come to care about these other things? You don't need the money. You need what Edgar has. Minus the decoys.

He went to a depressing Czech movie in the Village. Afterward he stopped for a steak and a beer at a local bar, then came home to his empty and small apartment and went to bed. And there, alone, he made the love of no goodbyes.

Lauren beat him in straight sets. Two, four, and love.

"You someplace else?" he asked and handed Spector an orange soda.

"Not yet. Or at least I'm not supposed to be gone yet. Sorry. I didn't give you a match out there."

"My pleasure. This is not for the glory of the sport. It's for the glory of my ego. Your trip on?"

"It's on." Spector reached inside his canvas duffel and pulled out six packets of envelopes. Stamped and addressed. He had added a mailing date to the labels.

"The crap I get," he said, "you can probably throw out. Or, if you don't want to bother, just toss it inside the door. I don't play the sweepstakes and no one has sent me money yet."

"You want to tell me where you'll be?"

"I don't know yet. I'll be in touch."

"I'm going to miss the games."

"Not if they're like today."

"Did we play today?"

Spector smiled. He enjoyed this man. He had never seen him other than in shorts and sneakers, he didn't know if he was honest or crooked, but he enjoyed him. They sat watching the sun drown in the New York haze, and Spector had a startling thought. If things went right, he'd soon have over a million dollars and not a clue of what to do with it.

"Lauren," he said.

His friend turned.

"I've been thinking about what you said. Connections. I need connections too. A different sort. I am unconnected."

"Sure. The hot-dog merger man of Wall Street? Don't give me that shit. I've seen your press."

That was the first time that Lauren indicated he knew anything about him. Spector liked that. He liked the recognition and equally liked Lauren's reserve.

"A different sort," he said again. "What I'm getting at is this. You know a potful about reinsurance. I know a potful about raising money. Maybe we ought to put what we know together. A potful in every pot."

"Meaning?"

"I may come into some money soon. It's connected with this trip. It would be a nice grubstake. Can you buy a healthy reinsurance company with a million dollars?"

"You putting me on? Cash U.S. greenies?"

"Cash."

"Oh, man, can you. Can you ever. With that down we can finance the rest of the purchase on the company's contracts. These companies get leveraged all the time. Might take a while to find the right one."

"Tell you what. You keep it in mind. Keep your eye out. I'll see if this deal comes through. Six months or so, maybe we'll look at doing something together. Deal?"

"Deal," said Lauren.

They walked out of the park and parted at the street. Spector felt better than he had in days.

He returned to Chicago with a single motive. The Empire interview had gone well and he needed no more research. He did have to pick up after the character of Roger Weedman, to make sure Weedman had left nothing behind. Still in Lake Forest were his clothes, files, the answering machine. The cats came and went on their own. Good thing they were self-sufficient.

After picking up the Parishes' Wagoneer he had left at the airport, Spector stopped at the market for a chicken, freshly butchered and quartered, and some vegetables. Nothing in plastic for our man Roger. He steered up the Parishes' winding drive in their Wagoneer. The fewer cabs the better. To welcome himself, he turned on all the lights, even those by the pool. He had passed up the airline meal, in anticipation of a celebration feast. He uncorked a good Amontillado sherry and poured a healthy glass. Then, from memory, he arranged all the ingredients on the counter, and put the chicken in the sink to drain. He spent twenty minutes on the sauce alone. He prepared enough for six.

What the hell, I can give any extra to the cats. How long can you eat those pebbles?

He chose two wines from a locker by the bar and put them both in the refrigerator to cool. He could decide later which to open. Never make a decision you don't have to.

He set the timer, opened the kitchen window so he'd hear it, and took his glass of sherry outside for a walk. It was eight o'clock and the darkness was settling in. The aromas from the wine and the garden blended.

What was the sound? It couldn't be rain, and the sprinklers were timed to run in the morning. Somewhere water was flowing. The Jacuzzi. He must have turned on the jets with the light switch. He walked over the flagstone path to the pools. I wonder if you have to go back in to turn them off?

The answer was no. In the Jacuzzi was a woman, holding on to the side and kicking lazily. His neighbor, the one from the shopping center. What was her name? Try as he might, he couldn't recall. His memory had been displaced—swallowed?— by that other part of his brain which had focused on her white and quite naked ass.

"Carol," she said, guessing at one cause of his distress.

"Hello," he said.

"We don't have one of these. I love them. I have the hots for your hot tub. Hope you don't mind."

"Oh, no," he said. He was not going to let her mute him again. "How's the water?"

"The water's fine. C'mon in. Or don't you feel like warming up?"

"It sounds just right."

The buzzer on the stove sounded. She looked at him.

"Dinner," he said and walked to the kitchen.

He clicked off the timer and removed the pan. The chicken looked ready, but a relaxing bath first would, somehow he felt sure, not diminish his appetite.

She came into the kitchen, in a blue terry-cloth robe. Terry cloth must be in among the Lake Forest set.

"What's for dinner?" she asked.

"Chicken." He was about to explain the recipe, then thought better of it. "Hungry?"

"Oh," she said and wet her lips with a darting pink tongue. She walked toward him, watching him with what he knew was intended as mystery and provocation. There was, of course, no mystery about it.

She put her arms around him and he felt the dampness of her body through the robe and his thin summer clothes.

"Oh, yes," she said. "I could eat a horse."

He could have sworn she ripped the sheets. When he looked, later, they were intact. Her nails running down them had made a ripping sound. Skating across his back, they had felt as if they were going through his skin as well. But he too was in one piece.

"I've always wanted to screw in Edgar and Lila's house. Trouble is, I didn't want Edgar."

He laughed.

"Are you here for the month, professor?"

"Not regularly," Spector said. "I'll be in and out."

"So I noticed," she said and laughed raucously.

They shared the chicken and he opened a bottle of Meursault. It had an exceptional taste. She didn't seem to notice. It was the highlight of his evening. He thought the sex was undistinguished.

She offered to do the dishes. He went to the rec room and put on the stereo system. *Hello Dolly.* Playing to the crowd. Was she, he wondered, a hazardous bed partner? Too late to worry. While not exactly a celibate, she was probably in a low-risk group. Life is a series of risks and rewards. Spector had never been meticulous about health risks, and hygiene always took a second to passion. Or boredom.

As he walked back, through Edgar's study, he noticed the answering machine showed two calls. He rewound the tape and hit Play.

A beep. A dialogue in Spanish. The voice of Guitterez, the Mexican banker, telling the U.S. operator that he would leave a message. Then his formal tones.

"The law firm of Sandoval and Sandoval, Panama City, expects your call and awaits your instructions. They will make arrangements to clear the funds through our bank. Since you come so highly recommended, we have waived our usual fee, but you understand we will have to use the current rates of exchange. Both to the peso and then to the Panamanian balboa. The arrangements for the fees of the lawyers you should make directly."

Numbers, country code and city code, for the firm of Sandoval and Sandoval. Spector copied it quickly. Two clips on moving the money. That will probably come to ten percent. Hell, Panama currency floated with the U.S. dollar. There was no rate of exchange. No fee indeed.

A beep. A second voice. Less self-conscious.

"Tony Urso, Ed. Friday afternoon, getting ready to leave for the long weekend. We're all set to take your loan to committee Wednesday. No hitches so far. Thought you'd want to know. Have a good day."

Was Urso disingenuous? Spector would listen again when he was alone. More carefully. If Urso were setting him up, would his voice reveal it? Could it really be this easy?

"What was all that?"

Carol Kittredge stood at the door, the last of the white wine in her glass.

Spector was stammering again. Some of the people he had invented had to go off on vacation. He could no longer keep track of them without name tags.

"I don't know," he said finally. "Probably for the Parishes. I write their messages down." Here he showed her the pad. "Otherwise the machine gets overloaded."

"I've never heard anyone ever call him Ed." She was skeptical.

"Maybe you've just never gotten to know him well enough." Spector gave her a broad wink and took her gently by the waist.

She laughed. It wasn't difficult to derail Mrs. Kittredge's train of thought.

He ushered her out the back door, promising to keep an eye on the Jacuzzi to see if she turned up again. She will have a long wait, he thought. I'd better set the timer or she'll be parboiled by October.

15

"Edgar. This is John Dixon at First Illinois. I have a Miss Olive on the phone, with your New York bank. Please call me to confirm delivery of securities from your custodial account."

It was a Tuesday, the day after Labor Day. Time was growing short. The call had come as Spector sat in the study, and the strange voice with its familiarity had startled him, started his heart pounding.

Spector listened to the tape twice. His first reaction was to bolt. Urso, or rather his exotic and thorough assistant, had ignored Spector's plea and had called Dixon without warning. The connection might have revealed the entire construct. But it hadn't. Dixon's flat voice was that of a perfunctory inquirer, with no tone of alarm or suspicion.

Look on the bright side. The note I signed as Parish has done its job: Dixon was not caught unawares. This call proved some hypotheses. For one, New York is corroborating facts on his application, arranging for transfer of the collateral. True, Dixon obviously knows Parish, and knows his voice. How many others at First Illinois do? Can I get this done without talking to Dixon? Spector played the tape a third time, then erased it.

On Labor Day he had made his international calls. Down at the shopping center, he called Panama City and the Registry of Births in Hamilton, Ontario.

In the first, he had arranged with the lawyers for their fees, the terms of the trusts, and for the code word to trigger disbursement. "La Paloma." He was amused by his choice. "The Pigeon." And in the long list of possibilities, who was it?

In the second, he had ordered a duplicate birth certificate, promising to send four dollars, Canadian, for the fee. Nothing else needed. No proof that Cyrus Feade had lost the original, that he could pay the four dollars, that he was in fact Cyrus Feade. Nice folks, those Ontarians. That would give him a genuine birth certificate and a forged passport, each in a different name. Just the sort of glitch that confirmed rather than denied. Perfection is simulation. Mistakes are life.

After his calls he shopped. Most of the school supplies were on sale for the holiday. Not so the two Fodor guides.

Now to deal with John Dixon. He had to have a response. Spector phoned First Illinois, asked for Dixon, and, when the man answered with his name, hung up.

The hour before noon took forever. He thumbed through the guidebooks, but wasn't concentrating. He didn't know what he was looking for. He put them down and walked aimlessly through the house. In the study he picked up a putter by the fireplace and hit practice balls across the carpet.

Finally it was twelve, ten after, quarter after.

Again he pushed the numbers of First Illinois. Do they still call that noise a "dial tone"? Shouldn't they change it to "punch tone"?

"Mr. Dixon's office."

"Is he in?"

"I'm sorry, he's out to lunch."

"Is this his secretary?"

"I'm sorry. She's out to lunch too."

Perfect.

"Damn."

"Can I help you?"

"My name is Edgar Parish. Mr. Dixon called, and I just got his message. Lila and I are off to New York. Would you leave word for him?"

"Of course, Mr. Paris."

"Parish. Like the priest. Listen, will you please tell him that he's authorized to do just what the Empire State people want. Tell him to send along the papers he needs, and I'll sign them at the New York closing. Got that?"

94

"Yes, sir."
"Good girl."

To protect the already injured desk, he covered its top with pages from the morning's *Tribune*. Then he laid out his tools in front of him: the modeling knife; the two small tubes which, their contents mixed, made an epoxy binding; a washcloth in a saucer; construction paper; four pens, all black; a caliper; and a spray can. It was like being in kindergarten again.

He took out the prized passport, and the two photos he had taken in O'Hare.

Squinting, he traced the knife around Feade's photo and eased it off the page. That paste wasn't water soluble; it too seemed to be a resin-based glue. But if you didn't hurry, if you were very careful, the denser cardboard could be separated without damage to the membrane of the paper. It worked. He put the old photo in the traveling garbage bag.

The inside cover of the passport listed Feade's name and statistics. He measured the distance between the branches on the capital "F" and recorded his finding. Then the full letter. With the knife he cut a stencil for each mark. After several tries, laying his product over the original, he had what he wanted.

Then he tested the ink. Washcloth in hand, he made faint marks on a separate page and compared quality. One pen showed a grain, but the remaining three were suitable. He chose the darkest. It would lighten after the plastic.

He placed his first stencil over the name and stroked. Then the second. Feade had become Reade. After the ink dried, he marked again, and sprayed the final product with clear laminate.

Carefully, he mounted his own picture in the passport. He pressed down the finished product, choosing from the ample shelves Bryce's two-volume work, *The American Commonwealth*. Edgar's father, it seemed, had been a bit of a scholar.

He thought of his own parents. When he was a senior in college, his father had contracted a disease that required costly and recurrent blood transfusions. That treatment and the hospitalization had used up most of his mother's savings, and he was torn throughout those months by conflicting rages: the anger at his father for so burdening his mother without adequate insurance or resources; the press of filial duty; the frustration that—

95

though well schooled and accomplished—he had no capability to earn enough money.

After his father's death, Spector determined to replace the savings. He did so in a matter of a few years. Was he competing with his father's ghost? To his disappointment, his mother was unimpressed with the feat. In place of the gratitude he expected, she bore a faint resentment toward the funds, which now appeared to her a cruel metonymy for a dead husband.

But by then Spector had committed himself. He had developed a knack for earning sums, large sums, and so he reflexively exercised it. Careers have sprung from more capricious circumstances. And its exercise led him to the choices that followed. Promotions, more money, marriage to Joan: she saw him as what he portrayed, what he had wanted his mother to see, an ambitious young man who carried a lot of baggage—a co-op, tailored clothes, tastes that needed feeding.

Spector lifted up the two books to check his handiwork. Some glue oozed from under the snapshot. He took the corner of the washcloth and mopped it clean.

Perhaps all I needed was a change. The thought pleased him and a smile eased his face. Perhaps I would have felt as satisfied if I'd become a carpenter or taken a job driving a bus. Is this life of crime a redundancy?

Nothing would surprise his mother more, he knew. Her expectations of him had wide political and social scope. She would take offense not if he became a fascist or a Bolshevik—her husband had been in sympathy with the latter, and she probably thought he was already the former. But in her moral views she shared none of her son's latitude, knew no one who did, and would not accept that her son had an interest in the literature of crime, never mind the act itself.

Included in the packages he had given to Lauren were four letters to his mother, full of plausible news. He had signed and stamped a birthday and a Christmas card. He would supplement the mail with an occasional call, from wherever it was he would be traveling.

The thought brought him back to the decision he must make. Cyrus MacNeil Reade wanted travel plans. The requirements: somewhere an American would not be conspicuous, with good banking technology to enable the transfer of funds, and where his languages—passable French and a combination of

Spanish and Italian that read menus in both—would get him by.

He leafed through the travel books. They didn't help. What is it like to live there? he thought. Six months, perhaps a year, until the money is washed. The books were of no help. Better go to literature. He liked many of the American expatriates. Hemingway, Baldwin, Henry James. None of them had moved to Hong Kong.

The phone rang. He waited for the machine to switch on, heard himself reading the greeting, and then the energetic voice of Tony Urso.

"Ed. Just want you to know. This package is set to go to loan committee tomorrow. If they approve, and I don't see that they can help it, we could be ready to close this thing by Friday. Hope that's fast enough service for you."

The machine clicked off. He rewound the tape and erased it. He had his hand on the phone and was about to call a number, then thought better of it. Phone logs were precise to the second. Someone could cross-check the time entry on a computerized reservation with the phone log and figure out where the call had originated.

He went to the garage and started up the Wagoneer. As he went down the Parishes' driveway, he saw Carol Kittredge roll into hers in a tan Mercedes sedan. He waved. The man in the seat next to her, thick clouded glasses and a face like a Mafia don's, waved back.

He drove the half-mile to the shopping mall, parked by the phone booth, and made the call.

After some talk and a wait, the voice came back to him.

"I can confirm that now. One first-class ticket Flight 595, for Monday, departs Dulles five-thirty P.M., arrives Geneva seven-forty-six A.M. Return open. And what is the name on that ticket?"

"R-e-a-d-e. Reade. First name Cyrus."

"Cash or credit card?"

"Cash. I'll pay when I pick it up."

"Then please allow an extra twenty minutes. Anything else we can do for you, Mr. Reade?"

"Not a thing."

"Very well. Thank you for flying Air France. And have a pleasant trip."

"*Merci, mademoiselle.* Thank *you*."

97

16

On Wednesday Spector packed up all traces of Roger Weedman, including an almost new telephone-answering machine, in a large black plastic garbage bag. He took a cab to the village and left the bag in a dumpster. A second cab picked him up by the shoe-repair store and took him to O'Hare. No need to hang around.

If the auditing process had turned up the revealing defect, and if he could detect any trace of suspicion in the voice of Tony Urso, he was prepared to resume the life he had been living until the time of his charade. Though, as the song says, who calls that living?

At LaGuardia the plane stacked up behind the usual queue of business traffic. After an interminable wait in the air and another on the ground for a gate to open, he deplaned and went to the nearest telephone.

"Mr. Urso, please."

"I'm sorry, he's in a meeting."

"Would you please tell him that Mr. Parish called and will call back this afternoon."

"Oh, Mr. Parish. Ms. Olive is here. Just a minute. I can connect you."

Not good. He preferred Urso, voluble, eager to please, expansive Urso. This exotic woman he couldn't read nearly so well. What was it about her that seemed incongruous?

"Mr. Parish. Or may I call you Ed as well?"

Her manner of speech put him off guard. It had a subtle beat of ambiguity. Was she flirting? Mocking? Entrapping?

"I wish you would," he said warmly.

"The committee considered your application this morning. It appears as if everything is in order."

Appears? What is she saying?

"You'll need to give us the account number at the Chemical, of course."

The Chemical. His mind raced through the Parish loan application. Did Edgar have an account there? Why is she asking this? Are they setting me up?

"The Chemical, Cynthia. I'm sorry, I'm not tracking."

"For the money."

"The money."

"You may remember there's some money involved. One million seven hundred thousand dollars. Less loan fees of about one-half percent. You *are* going to make that investment, aren't you?"

He caught on. The units for the restaurants. He had paid them little attention. The private placement memo called for the funds to be deposited in the partnership account at the Chemical Bank.

"Of course. The Chemical. Yes, yes. The account number. So the loan has been approved."

"So far, so good. Unless you show up at closing with a mask and a gun."

No need.

"Not my style, Cynthia."

"I didn't think so. We'll close Friday, ten o'clock, at the bank. If that's convenient for you."

"That's fine. Couldn't be better. I'm in New York now."

"Where are you staying?"

"I have no reservations. I just got off the plane." That much was true. "You have any suggestions?" He meant a half-jest, and was unhappy with the way it came out.

She ignored the question.

"Will Mrs. Parish be coming to the closing?"

"No. She's traveling. Right after this trip I'm going to join her."

"Europe?"

"No," he said guardedly. What is she getting at? "Hong Kong."

"Well," she said, coming to some conclusion he couldn't guess at. "All alone in the big city. Stay out of trouble."

"Oh, I will. At least until Friday."

"See you then."

He went directly to his apartment. No need for a hotel address. Lauren had been diligent about taking in the mail, and had left a note scribbled on the back of a flyer for a dry cleaner's:

> May be on to something. Give me a call when
> you're ready to look. Lauren

I can put a million in a business, he thought. I'll have enough to pay taxes, and have some pocket money left over. Assuming I don't take too close of a haircut along the way.

What did the call with Cynthia mean? He couldn't tell, could hear no suspicion. It was that damned coyness, that sparring that he didn't associate with the usual banker-debtor relationship.

Spector brought himself down to the mundane business details. He called an old college classmate, now a corporate lawyer practicing downtown, and explained his problem. He intended to start a new company, Spector Peripherals. He would be capitalizing it with just enough to pay legal bills, which he wanted to keep to a minimum. He had a new slant on selling services to companies interested in changing over their peripheral alignment. He was going to take it abroad. If it didn't work, he'd be back in six months. If it worked, he'd sell it as soon as he could. He wanted all long-term capital gain at the end. No ordinary income. One never knew what Congress would do to the laws. He was prepared to pay his taxes, but only once.

He answered the lawyer's questions. No customers in the U.S., and no office or employees here either. Probably doing business in Switzerland. Maybe the U.K. also. No employees. No other stockholders. As simple as possible.

"You know what you want," said the friend.

Only in the irrelevancies, he thought.

"The best structure for you would be an offshore company. One in the country where you're going to be doing business. Or an OPEC country. That way you pay the least amount in qualification fees. Your taxes will depend on the specific jurisdiction—on that score, I'd suggest Great Britain, since you fit into their entrepreneurial incentive plan. You'll pay only U.K. Inland

Revenue taxes, and claim a credit on your U.S. tax return. When you sell, you'll pay U.S. taxes on the gain. These are good years to take large gains. Rates are down."

"Sounds fine. What do we do next?"

"You contact a London solicitor. Tell him what I've told you. He'll do the rest."

"Look. I'm in a bit of a rush. Can you do all that for me? Assure him I'm a responsible person, not a bank robber. Have him set the whole thing up. I'll be in touch with him."

"Be happy to." His friend gave him the name of the solicitor and his firm, one of the City's oldest, housed in the shadow of Saint Paul's Cathedral. That piece was in place. It pays to hire responsible help.

For the closing that Friday, Spector eschewed the yellow jacket. He had left it in the dumpster in Lake Forest, together with his other ersatz Parish clothes. He wore an old suit of his, from before he'd bothered with Savile Row tailors. Yet he could not rid himself of his studies of Meyerhold and the empirical bases of acting. And so he had taken a tie from Edgar's closet. On it three ducks flew, their contrails framing an elegantly stitched marsh. And this Friday he put it on.

It was a talisman, he thought, a good-luck charm. But the thought didn't soften his embarrassment. It was, after all, Edgar's.

At Cynthia's suggestion, Spector had opened an account for Edgar Parish at Chemical. If all went well, Empire State would deposit the loan proceeds there, he would wire them that day to Banco Nacional in Mexico City, and he would then let his Panama connections know that the pigeon had landed. The money, net of the bites taken as it traveled across the border and down the isthmus to the land Cortés had called Darién, would be locked in anonymity by this afternoon. If all went well. The process reminded Spector of the old man in the Hemingway book, his mythic catch lashed to his boat, trying to gain shore before the meat was gone.

Spector took a deep breath and entered the Empire State Bank for the second and last time. He wanted to see as few people as possible, and so he rode the elevator directly to the third floor and asked for Mr. Urso. You're here for the closing, said the receptionist, and he admitted he was. Ominous word, that, he thought.

She led him to a different room. He had visualized the scene of the closing several times, in an attempt to anticipate its sequence. Now, when the setting had changed, he was troubled. But not as much as he was to be by the addition to the cast.

Urso was first to his feet to greet him.

"You know Miss Olive."

Spector let his eyes rest on that lovely sight for only a second. She was dressed this day in a tan summer dress, with a scarf around her neck that hid her perfect neck and instead reflected it reds and greens into her face.

Caribbean. Maybe Mexican. Who was this exotic woman, and did she belong with the bank? Or was he the victim of some correlative hoax? He was being introduced to the third person in the room and knew he had to pay attention.

". . . Herbert Orton . . . examiner's office."

"With whom?"

"The state bank examiner's office."

"Is there something the matter?" He had no back door today. Everything was going so well, he had forgotten about getting out. A confession? He'd gone too far for that to be of much help.

Urso ignored his question. "Mr. Orton would like to sit in on this closing, with, of course, your permission."

"Well," Spector said, "frankly, I feel my financial matters are my own business. No offense, Mr. Orton."

"Certainly, Ed. Certainly. They are. But the state office by law has a right to all our records, and that includes all the documents you've left with us." Urso was clearly eager for Spector to pass on this, and Spector could not yet tell whether he had cause, beyond his insecurities, to be alarmed.

"What is the purpose of this, Mr. Orton?"

"Part of our new procedures, Mr. Parish. It is Mr. Parish? Since we comment on the adequacy of loan documentation after transactions are completed, the commissioner felt it might be helpful for us to audit an occasional transaction before completion. It's a new procedure."

Aside from his full and neatly squared mustache, Orton looked like Wally Cox. Probably why he grew the mustache.

"Fine," said Spector. "Let's proceed."

Spector had attended dozens of commercial closings, maybe hundreds. He was put off neither by the stacks of papers nor by the snail's pace. He knew the one single and signal point of the psychology of these ceremonies: once the money changes hands, so does all the leverage.

He listened as Cynthia Olive explained each form: revised loan applications, FTC disclosure documents, waivers of rescission period, conditional assignments, verification and instruction on collateral. Ah, there was the signature of John Dixon. It revived Spector, like a shipwrecked sailor who spots the floating branch of a tree. He took each document from her hand, with its long fingers and tomato-red nails, and appeared to read it. In practice, it didn't matter what recondite terms were there. If they asked for the keys to his house or three hours with Lila as maiden rights, he was prepared to sign.

Cynthia explained. Her face was earnest; her eyes were on his. He watched her, noticed how many shapes the mouth made, where the tongue went with every vowel sound.

Finally they were there. He was presented with the promissory note. He looked it over, grumbled about the rate of interest, and signed it. By now writing Parish's name came easily.

"Just a minute," said Orton.

They looked up, all startled.

Orton opened his hard Samsonite case. He took out three pages, stapled at the corner.

What was it? Spector thought. A description of the real Edgar Parish, furnished by First Illinois? The list of actual investors in that restaurant deal? A verification of Social Security numbers?

Spector peered over the table but couldn't make it out. They sat in silence, waiting. Was each one, as Spector was, considering what he had at risk? Cynthia, several days' work. Urso, a commission, part of a profit plan. He, three to five years in a federal penitentiary.

Orton spoke.

"I don't see here the minutes of the loan committee."

They looked at him blankly. He repeated his sentence.

"Oh," said Cynthia. "I'll get them. We don't generally have them present at the closing."

"Our procedures are they should go in the loan closing file," Orton said primly.

"They will, Mr. Orton. But we don't have them here. I'll get you a copy." She shot him a look that said, Give me a chance and you'll forget about the minutes. Orton acknowledged that he could get a copy later.

He checked his list again. Everything else was, he seemed to begrudge, in order.

Cynthia explained the wiring procedures to them, and Spector agreed. Confirmation would come in about an hour, if he wanted to stay. No need, he would check later. She began stacking the papers they had generated.

"You're serious about your work."

"I'm serious about money," she said, not looking up.

"Your own as well as other people's?"

"I don't have much of my own," she said, "yet." She glanced at him and allowed her lips to stay parted an instant longer.

"Now that I have all this," he said, holding the wire-transfer order aloft, "let me take you to dinner."

"That isn't yours. It's ours. Remember?" She passed his invitation without acknowledging it.

Urso, somewhat ill at ease, rose to leave. They stood up as well. Spector shook hands with Urso and asked Cynthia to walk him to the door.

"Is there anything else I can get for you?" she asked.

An envelope. Addressed to him at his Lake Forest address. He wanted to mail his set of papers so he wouldn't have to carry them abroad. She dispatched a secretary.

As they were waiting by the elevator, she said, "I don't know that I've ever seen anyone as interested in what I was saying. You must get off on Truth-in-Lending regulations."

"I was thinking," he said, "what fun it would be to be that scarf."

She lowered her head and gave him a reproving but not unfriendly smile.

"And you a solid, married suburbanite. You're not what you seem, Mr. Parish."

The secretary handed her the envelope addressed and stamped. The elevator came. He let it go.

"Have dinner with me tonight. To celebrate."

She looked at him a moment. That moment was as charged, as erotic, as any Spector had spent in bed.

"Do you think you can find Brooklyn?"

"You go to Chavez Ravine and take a left."

She took the envelope from under his arm and a pen from his suit pocket, wrote down an address, and handed both back to him.

"Pick me up at seven," she said, "and book a table at the River Cafe." She turned and walked away.

Not a bad day's work. A million seven and an evening with the most exciting woman he had met since . . . when? Joan? He had never had this sense of exotica with her. There was something streetwise about Cynthia, something about her that had nothing to do with interest rates, lenders, and borrowers.

He found himself at the corner of Fifty-seventh and Park. He noticed a mailbox. Traffic and pedestrians streamed by. None of them thought it untoward when a handsome young man carrying a stack of papers undid his tie, put it in an envelope, and mailed it back to its owner.

17

He was there early, and he waited in the cab until his watch showed seven straight up. She lived in a rehab brownstone in Park Slope, an area of Brooklyn that had slipped from the surface of society to several fathoms under, and now, with the shortage of Manhattan space for any but the richest and poorest, was inflating with developers' dollars and rising again.

Her apartment was on the third floor. She answered the door and didn't invite him in. She wore a simple black skirt and a loosely knit black cotton sweater. It had a wide but modest vee neck, thin off-the-shoulder sleeves. Around her neck, the neck that like a Brancusi marble you needed to touch, she wore a single strand of pearls. Good pearls. Her clothes emphasized the blackness of her eyes, a deeper color than black, a deeper luster. It wasn't happenstance.

"You approve?" she said, without sarcasm.

"I approve."

The cab pulled up in front of the River Cafe.

It had not been easy. And, more to the point, it was a senseless risk. No one could get into the River Cafe on such short notice, even in the summer. But he had called in his chits on this one. He had found Walter, the maître d', told him he wanted a window table for two, seven-thirty, no nonsense. Reminded Walter of the merger celebrations he had paid for, when the Veuve Cliquot never stopped, when the tips weren't computed on some recommended percentage in a tourist's guide to New York and, more important, were in cash. Walter obliged.

And Walter was the risk.

They walked in. Spector was relieved to find that seating guests was a young woman, not his acquaintance. She showed them to a table flush by the window, with an uninterrupted view of the harbor.

"Oh," she said. He thought it the first spontaneous syllable she had uttered.

"You approve?"

"I approve," she said.

They sat and watched the sun go down in New Jersey. The lights of lower Manhattan came on. The water of the river, its nastiness unknowable in the elegance and gathering dark of the moment, lapped against the barge five feet from their elbow.

Their dinner was memorable. Veal pounded to the thinness of a piecrust with capers and pimiento, scallops served raw in lime juice and rosemary, a duck whose liquor had been blended with the Benedictines'. All the excesses of a grand culture running short of ways to amuse itself. Cynthia had never been there before, and though her first line of defense was a tough carapace, she softened to the romance of the food, the wine, the pampering.

"How is it you knew the name of the restaurant you wanted to go to?"

"I keep a list in mind where I want to go next. In case someone asks."

"And you had no hesitation going out with a bank customer?"

She didn't think about that for long. "You seemed interesting. Trustworthy." With that she tilted her head and looked at him quizzically. He smiled, but not at what she could know.

"Cynthia Olive, you are a realist. You take people as they seem. And seeming is all that matters."

How could she possibly suspect? She could not. Is she trying to coax something from me? he wondered.

She answered him. "A realist isn't one who takes people as they seem. That's a moron. I merely understand that someone may seem one way and indeed be that way."

He had nothing to say about Parish and his past: he saw nothing flattering in the portrait that she had of him—unemployed, rich, idle. So he kept to world views, funny comments on the two people they knew in common, Orton and Urso. Finally he inquired about her.

She had, he thought, a most remarkable story. She was born Cynthia Oliveras. Her mother was Greek, her father Puerto Rican. She grew up at 136th Street and Lenox Avenue.

"That's Harlem," he said blankly.

"That's Harlem, baby."

Her mother sent her to the sisters from the time she could go to school and threatened her with eviction if she didn't pay attention.

"Most of my friends were out on the streets or living with a man by the time they were fifteen. If my old lady had waited a few years to make that threat," Cynthia told him, "I would have thought it was an invitation."

After graduating from the Carmelites, she spent a year as a secretary in a downtown law firm.

"It was like coming to religion. I saw things I'd never even heard of. Don't get the idea I was a nun. By high-school graduation I knew more positions from the Kama Sutra than stations of the cross. But this is a world, man, I never seen."

She looked up from her asparagus. "Am I shocking you, Mr. Parish?"

"No." He smiled. When she went back in time, she went back in diction. And he could hear in her voice the clicking of the Puerto Rican accent, so carefully stowed until now.

"Never seen before. I mean, these cats live in Connecticut and Greenwich and Sutton Place. And the wives go to those stores I've only seen ads for. All the time.

"So I figure, I'll cut me in. They have this program for the staff, continuing education. You got to be there ten years or something. But the guy who runs it, he's a young guy, married but a young guy, and they're always staying in town to work late. I mean, it couldn't have been easier.

"So I'm back at school. City University. First at night, but I do so well they give me money. Everyone wants a spic to help, especially one who won't knife you. Pretty soon I've graduated, in business administration, and I'm a trainee at Empire State."

She took a bite of duck and a sip of wine.

"I think it's remarkable," Spector said.

"Funny. That's what the guy at the firm said. You're a lot like him." She shot Spector an unmistakable look. He was at a negotiating disadvantage, the one every primer on the subject said to avoid. She knew what he wanted, but he hadn't a glimmer. It was odd. He didn't the least bit mind.

They split a brandied soufflé and drank espresso. Her eyes shone black against the refracted light.

The dinner was over. When the bill came, she asked to see it, and for the second time uttered a few unguarded words:

"Oh, shit," she said softly. "That's a week's pay for me. After taxes."

"Not for long, I'd guess." It was the one compliment he could have paid her, and she was pleased.

They walked to the door. A perfect evening. There, watching them advance, was Walter. Spector put his finger to his lips. In vain.

"Everything all right, Mr. Spector?"

"Everything was wonderful. Thank you."

As he had asked, a cab was waiting on the cobblestones.

"What did he call you? He seemed to know you."

"I must look like a lot of people. Happens to me all the time. One of these days I'll get shot by a jealous husband."

"And he'll have a good chance of being right."

She had paid back the compliment in kind. He took her arm.

The cab pulled up in front of her place.

"I'd love to see your apartment," he said. He had forgotten whether it was Spector or Parish who would try to go to bed with her, and he had forgotten how each would go about it.

"I'll bet."

What the hell does that mean? He paid the driver and sent him off, then followed her up the stairs. She opened the front door with her key, and they walked up the two flights.

She poured them each a drink. A finger of Scotch with a lone ice cube. It wasn't appetizing, but, then, he didn't feel like drinking.

The living-room walls were decorated with posters, framed and unframed. They sat on the sofa, each in the elbow of its curve, facing each other.

"You look awkward," she said.

"What a seductive thing to say."

"Here." She straightened around and patted her lap. "Put your head here."

He knew he should be getting on. He was unsure what it was she wanted of him, and some part of him feared that it was the truth. He took off his jacket and lay it over the ample couch. Slowly he swiveled where he sat and lay down with his head on her thigh. He felt the temperature of the leatherlike fabric beneath him and the temperature of her body.

She put her fingers lightly on his brow. Instinctively he closed his eyes, and lighter still she ran her fingertips over the closed lids. They fluttered under her touch.

"You're jumpy."

"I'm high-strung."

"Nervous?"

"Yes."

"About the loan closing?"

"About the loan closer."

She laughed a throaty laugh. Slowly she began to massage the bones about the eyes. His back unknotted. He felt as if he had fallen in space. It was that elusive time. That moment he knew was coming had come, that resolution of a theme from somewhere beyond memory, somewhere different. It was in his recollected fantasies, the conclusion of what he had wanted, then forgotten.

Her fingers worked under the eyebrow.

"There's a spot . . ." she said, ". . . here. Where just by pressing you can release all tension. Even pain."

He felt himself falling further.

"What are you doing to me?"

"Shiatsu. The Japanese art of massage."

She worked in silence. "Here's a place that relaxes the lower back and"—she hesitated—"between the legs."

It was so. He felt the seam of his body stretch.

"You're casting a spell over me."

"What sort of spell?"

He was silent for several minutes. If it was true, he didn't want to change it.

"Morgause was one of the three charmed sisters of Cornwall. When she wanted to capture King Arthur," he told her, "she used a spancel, a magical tape. You need the body of a soldier, a young soldier. From it you must remove the narrowest strip of skin, and then only the top layer. A tape, almost a thread. Start at the shoulder, go down the outside of the right arm, around the edge of each finger. Then follow around the entire outline of the body, as if you were tracing it. The entire body. You finish with a long, fragile tape."

She was tracing the outline of his fingers, like the seam of a glove.

"Once you had it, you used it as a lariat. If there were someone you wanted to fall in love with you, you found him while he slept and you threw it over his head. If he didn't awaken, he was bound to fall in love with you within the week."

"And if he woke up?"

"He would die."

She laughed, a deep sound in the back of her throat. Cynthia did not easily buy life-or-death romances, but she was charmed by his story.

He lay there inert in her lap. The world of the day had turned, as if he had circled the moon, and a world of sensation had slipped beneath them in its place. She brought him back with a question.

"Who are you?"

"What do you mean?"

He could not have moved to escape a falling sky, but some other part of him, not as agile as his mind, raced over discovery and alibi.

"Who are you? You're not the silly rich kid from Lake Forest that shows up in the loan papers."

"Oh, but I am. Why do you say that?"

"You're more like me."

"And who are you, Cynthia Olive?"

"For starters, not Cynthia Olive, remember?"

"I remember."

"Changed my name, and if that's not enough, I'll even change the way I strut my stuff."

"Your stuff is just fine. Whatever you do, don't change your stuff."

She seemed so casual about love, so earnest about work. Probably a function of which is in shorter supply.

"And as a serious career woman, you've given up on romance."

"I've given up on unrequited romance," she answered. "Then again, the world works in strange ways. That torrid affair with the young associate at the law firm? My Chappaqua massa. Out of that came two Cartier Christmases, a taste for good food, and eventually my job in loan operations. I'm requited."

He remained lying in her lap. The rubbing had stopped. So had the freedom from apprehension. They returned in tandem. He wondered what it was she wanted from him, and he opened his eyes to inquire of hers.

He found nothing in her face to tell him, only its slight, gentle smile.

"You're not enjoying the massage."

"I was."

"Maybe this will help."

She put her hand on his eyes, closing them. Then he sensed her lean forward and pull off her sweater, unhook her bra. Her hand returned to his head, this time to his temple, then his ear. Her finger traced around his chin and lightly drew the crest of his lips. He opened his eyes again, to see her, to see the breathtaking sculpture of her, broken only by that single strand of

111

pearls. He could not help but think of its provenance. Was it one of the two Christmas gifts? A subsequent bank customer? He didn't care. By the seeking in his eyes he asked for her body, and she brought it to him.

18

He stayed the night. And the day after. And the night and its following day too. Cynthia was happy to have him, and if not she never said the contrary. Spector felt buoyed, airy. He had always suspected strong feelings, because they weighed you down. These few days he was freed, weightless.

He had anticipated the joys of her remarkable and knowing body. She was uninhibited, inventive without seeming gymnastic. And she pleased herself at the same feast. If he had speculated, he would have seen that. But he was surprised by the undeserved intimacy. After his months of solitude it fell on him like rain on the desert. As with all egotists, living alone did not suit him, and he had begun to dislike his shabby and sullen bachelorhood.

Sometime in the dark of that first night—for nights, tastes, flesh all had merged into one memory—they were awake and he said, Tell me a secret. And she said, When you love me like that I want to be a man. I want to be you loving me. And she said, Your turn. And he said, For ten years after I was sixteen, everything I did was in order to get women. At sixteen I lifted weights, at eighteen taught tennis to browning ladies at a country club, at twenty memorized Rimbaud—Where am I? he said, and she said, Twenty—at twenty-two smoked a lot of hash, at twenty-four was a boy genius, at twenty-six put it all on one roll and it came up sevens. Then I got married and it all stopped. She said to him, Now give me some advice, and he said, Forget this happened. And he said, Your turn, and she said, Make familiar moves. Then they slept again.

When he awoke that Saturday morning he remained still, looking at this strange dark woman. She lay with her black hair falling over her face and the string of pearls still at her throat. He sensed about her not only the fragrance of their own love-making but that of the dozens, perhaps hundreds of his predecessors in this bed. And he was calmed by the absence of anxiety, of jealousy. Was it because he must leave? he wondered. The thought moved his insubstantial reflections, like a wind on a feather.

He considered their conversations of the night. Had he said anything stupid, anything revealing? If so, she didn't seem to notice.

In his eagerness for their dinner date, he had all but forgotten the money. Lying at her side, reflecting on the events that had brought them together, he remembered. Late Friday afternoon he had called Chemical and received confirmation that $1,691,500, the full loan after fees, had been received in the account of Edgar M. Parish and had been wired to Banco Nacional, Mexico City. He sent a telex to Mexico City authorizing disbursement and a companion telex to Panama, announcing that the corpus of the trust would be arriving, signing it Paloma. He had not heard from London about the formation of his new company. Because the time difference worked against him, he would have to wait until Monday morning.

There was something on his agenda for Saturday. What was it?

Christ. The flight.

He rose gingerly from the bed, slipped on his trousers, and went into the kitchen to make a call. The day had arrived. Air France confirmed that he could cancel, and they rescheduled Mr. Reade for the same flight, Dulles to Geneva, Monday afternoon. He found the coffee, filled the four-cup maker on the counter, and quartered two oranges. Then, loading a tray which he finished with a geranium cropped from a window box, he returned to find Cynthia on the cusp of morning.

He greeted her silently with a light kiss, and held out the coffee. Holding the sheet to her chin, she sat up and took a sip while he held the mug.

"Fresh coffee, oranges à la locker room. Limited menu."

She laughed.

"It's all I eat anyway." She nuzzled his arm and licked his bicep.

He thought of a question he had missed in the activity.

"Tell me," he said. "Why me?"

"What do you mean?"

"Why a married man, living far away. No real future. You don't strike me as being hard up for friends. And I'll pay back my loan anyway."

She laughed. "You want it straight?" she asked.

"Straight."

"You're handsome. Well built, sexy. You couldn't take your eyes off me. All that counts."

"And?"

"And you're in the right class. I gave up bedding poor men years ago. Now I'm moving out of middle management. I don't have many more years of picking and choosing. But so long as I do, I want to see how the aristocracy lives. How they do it."

"Am I aristocracy?"

"Anybody walks into a bank, signs his name, walks out with a million, that's aristocratic enough for me."

"And?"

"Up with the aristocracy." So saying, she took his hand and assured that her words came true.

Had he abandoned his plan? He had certainly suppressed it. If he could give back the money and have Cynthia, which would he choose? It was a useless speculation. He had no choice. Prosecuting attorneys and the Federal Bureau of Investigation took, he guessed, a skeptical view of romantic epiphanies.

The weekend was wonderful, made the better for his decision to forget about its ineluctable end. They did the things young lovers do in New York. They walked through expanses of Prospect Park, a block away from her apartment. They spent Sunday in the north end of Manhattan. At Saint John the Divine they watched a man carving saints out of limestone, fed peacocks in the garden. He walked her through the massive cathedral. She was unimpressed that it was second in size only to the Basilica in Rome, but she marveled that after 101 years its completion was not in sight.

"Can you imagine if you were the contractor waiting to get paid at the end of the job?"

They went farther north, to the Cloisters. He talked about their design and how as a kid he really wanted to be an architect. She didn't like the subjunctive, she said. The sisters had taught her that verbs of hoping or wishing take the subjunctive. She'd decided, she told Spector, to avoid those verbs. What she liked most was that the Cloisters were an imitation, a forgery.

"I never thought of it that way."

"What difference, if it's as good as the real thing?"

"What difference indeed."

She showed him the block where she had grown up. She didn't want to get out of the cab.

"Nothing to see. Just poor people."

She had a dozen records that he owned. The jazz, none of the classical. Monk, Pres, Lady Day. That's the way to match people up, he said. Keep a computer run on the music people buy. When you get to twenty records that she has, bam, you're hitched. Joan had liked Schoenberg. He told her not even Mrs. Schoenberg liked Schoenberg. Joan didn't think it was funny.

It was Sunday night. He was wearing jeans, sandals, and a pale-green tee shirt that said "Big Apple" on it. He had bought everything at the local chain store, except the shirt. That he borrowed from her. He used her toiletries, and they suited him fine. He could have gone to his apartment but he didn't want to take her and he didn't want to be without her.

He lay on the Naugahyde sofa in the living room, listening to the music. She sat on the floor beside him. On the wall were bullfight posters and, hanging by the one, light-starved window, falling spider plants in hemp saddles. Billie Holiday was singing.

"She a friend of yours?" he asked.

"An old friend. That's my theme song."

> *Them that's got shall get,*
> *Them that's not shall lose.*
> *So the Bible said,*
> *And it still is news.*

"Cynthia."

She stirred.

"You're really going to make it at the bank, aren't you?"

"You bet your ass."

He was silent a minute.

"I hope I haven't hurt your chances."

"Hurt? No way. They think you fell into their laps. They're delighted to find you."

"Yeah."

> Poppa may have,
> Momma may have,
> But God bless the child that's got his own,
> That's got his own.

"Anyway, I want to tell you how special these days have been. I wish to hell it didn't have to end."

"Everything ends, man." Again that street patois, scornful of the soft romanticism not everyone could afford.

"I guess so."

"Look. I took this on. I didn't expect you to leave Lila and the Lake Forest Yacht Club."

He laughed. "There is no Lake Forest Yacht Club." At least I don't think so.

"Not to worry, Edgar." She used his name only to tease him. "No broken hearts."

"I wasn't worrying about yours."

They kissed, tenderly and finally.

On Monday morning he caught a cab to his neighborhood, walking the last blocks just in case. You never knew. Television cops always caught people by checking cab records. He was packed in half an hour, and out the door for the airport. He had planned for, designed, built, and paid for the launch of his new life. It had not occurred to him that, once launched, he would not want to board.

Lake Geneva

19

Montreux. The ancient and popular town lies at the eastern end of Lake Geneva. The old city, an uphill walk from downtown, is a favorite with the many tourists who come for the music festival, only to find that their fondness for Brahms is no greater than it had been in Cincinnati. One can wander through the quiet, crooked lanes by the pastel houses. At one corner, standing on the cobblestones and viewing the vineyards on the hills beyond, the stroller has a view of four hundred years. From another corner, he looks down into the modern city.

Descending again toward the lake, often misted and gray, he passes cheesemakers, patisseries, and, as he nears the grand hotels by the lakeshore, glitzy boutiques and restaurants. He crosses the boulevard to put the town behind and stands on the quayside, that wide corso that fringes the lake itself for the entire perimeter of Montreux and into the suburbs.

Here on the promenade, one out for a walk need not feel conspicious about his solitude. It is a place for leisurely intercourse, a place where one needs no companion and no destination. To assimilate, one merely smiles at the visitors with their maps, phrase books, and coupons. One will soon be asked to take the picture of the visiting couple with the Castle of Chillon as a backdrop. During the day it is mostly tourists who stroll and sample the food at the cafés. In the evening resident and visitor share the walk, and young people come from the city and the neighboring towns, to look for each other and to roller-skate recklessly among the crowds. In the summer the foliage is that of a warmer clime: magnolias in bloom, fig and palm trees. The evenings are lit by the streetlamps above. Looking across the lake, one thinks for a moment he sees Montreux's reflection when indeed he is looking at the bobbing lights of boats and distant lamps from towns on the opposite shore.

In the warm evenings of September one can dress lightly, can still feel that he is strolling through a Renoir street scene. And, in the semidarkness, one can feel the warmth of human company, can feel less alone.

And here, to the quay, Spector came in the evenings to walk.

His days were spent at the house he had rented in nearby Vevey. There his time went to reading, bicycling, gardening, doing the paperwork necessary to complete the circular tale he had started. He had taken up gardening to get himself outdoors. The house had a small but successful garden, a small plot for vegetables and then roses, asters, mums. Nothing elaborate. The rental agent was delighted that Spector wanted to putter about, and simply sent the maintenance man around once a week to assure the tenant had not drowned the asparagus or induced a blight.

It pleased Spector that Vevey was the town of Courbet and Rousseau, both fugitives and radicals. And that for Chaplin's last years it was the city of refuge in his exile from the overheated political climate of the United States. Chaplin had been a hero to Spector's parents. An internationalist. America was shocked that he would leave his country of choice, surrender his wife's passport, consort with Russian and Chinese communists. But his parents understood. It was Mill's dream of a transnational humanism. They also knew that political nonconformity was a luxury of the rich—they couldn't afford it—and they admired Chaplin for indulging it.

On landing in Geneva, Spector had rented a car and driven around until he found a quiet, commodious setting. Geneva was gray and urban; Montreux was full of Americans. Like the little bear's porridge, Vevey was just right. The house was small. It had two bedrooms, a large central room, its bay window overlooking the lake, that served as a combined dining room and library, and that had walls lined with overspilling bookshelves. Most of the books were in French. But, with a good Larousse and a diligence he hadn't used since college, Spector resolved to rejuvenate his vocabulary. A few paperbacks were in German, and after one look at that intimidating language, he ignored them. And the owner, a Swiss national who came down from Basel for the summers, had a supply of novels in English.

The house was set back into the woods. A steep path led down the hill to the edge of a pedestrian right of way, with one lane reserved for cyclists. Where the path intersected, the owner had built a small log storage-shed, and in it was a rickety bicycle. The combination for the lock was posted on the kitchen wall, but the lock was left ajar, for only a desperate traveler would have stolen this relic. Spector became a daily sight, riding in the morning as the ubiquitous mists floated up from the lake's surface and vaporized in the last heat of September. Do they call it Indian summer too?

He had rented the house, and the car, in his own name, using the Spector passport and Spector-issued traveler's checks. He assumed that the Reade passport was "hot," and that it would be better if the passport number, even under a different name, appeared on no compilations. Hotels submitted passport information weekly. Rental agents might also.

All other purchases he made in cash. In several transactions, he moved his money from Panama to just down the highway at Geneva, where he had two numbered accounts at Crédit Suisse. True, those accounts were in the name of Cyrus MacNeil Reade, but under Swiss law a bank would protect the identity of a depositor unless there were proof of a felony against that name. And though one set of authorities were looking for Roger Weedman and a second for the chap who had run off with a passport of Cyrus Feade, there was nothing to link them together.

Now he needed to finish the circle, and for that he needed the Reade persona for one last arc. He gave the rental agent his real name over the phone, instructing him that the house would be occupied for most of the six months by his brother-in-law, a Canadian. That would be fine, so long as Monsieur Spector realized that the house was quite small, not suitable for more than two. And that Monsieur Spector would be held financially responsible for the tenancy. Monsieur Spector was aware.

Six months. The prospect of it seemed endless. He had some plans, but he didn't need half a year. His remaining task was to wash the money, now in Reade's name, so that it could be repatriated into the United States and used in his own name. It was for that purpose that he had created Spector Peripherals. Once he added some correspondence, files, and books of account, the company would be ready for use. He as sole owner would sell its stock for a check from Cyrus Reade, pay his taxes on the gain, and have clean, after-tax dollars sitting in a New York account in his own name. Painful as the taxes were to pay, they were a reasonable price for peace of mind. In that assessment, Spector felt he made the decision most citizens make.

He started a disbursements ledger using actual expenses. The car and house payments could easily be defended as serving a legitimate business purpose. It was in creating a receipts ledger that he let his fancy wander. Odd. An Internal Revenue agent will mercilessly root out false expenses, but he couldn't imagine any of them worrying about false income. So he set about his task with an entrepreneur's enthusiasm and rewarded the company generously. Spector Peripherals demanded earnings, even fictive earnings, if it were to become the subject of an acquisition that netted its owner over one million dollars.

He had time to burn. It occurred to him that he actually could start a company in his leisure, but for the fact that he couldn't risk failure. And the added fact that he knew nothing about peripherals. That made the risk high.

And so he rode his bike, entered numbers in his ledgers, dusted his roses, and in the evening drove the eight or ten kilometers to Montreux to walk on the promenade and hear the voices. The music festival was in its last days, and though there were programs of Mozart and Telemann and Bach, he absented himself. He did not want to run into an acquaintance from one of his increasing number of past lives.

He tried to read from the novels in the house. He was halfway through Hawthorne's *Blithedale Romance*, chosen because of its title, when he discovered he had no idea of what was going on and no interest in finding out. There was nothing relevant there, nothing of the flesh and irreverence and heat of Cynthia. He replaced it on the shelf and took down *Treasure Island*.

Only a month had gone by. He remembered a story he had read—was it Poe or de Maupassant?—about a young man who goes to his fiancée's burial. He is so overcome by grief that he loses himself in reverie and remains behind in the crypt after it is sealed. He quickly douses the candles to conserve air, and determines that, if he can keep himself alive, eventually he will be missed in the village and rescued. With this hope he sets a routine for himself, of exercise, sleep, meditation. His only food source is the candles. He divides each in thirds and determines to eat one of the six pieces each day. It is pitch dark, he has no measure of the passing days, and he is alone with his thoughts of grief and survival. Finally, after he has eaten three of the pieces of paraffin, he is rescued. His friends listen to his story, but they do not understand his despair: they realized immediately what had happened and came to free him. He had been in the crypt only two hours.

No, Spector thought. I will not make it for six months without some contact. He reached for the Fodor's guide he had brought all the way from Lake Forest, found Montreux in the index, and began searching for a suitable restaurant to visit that very evening.

In Vevey it was five o'clock, early for dinner. In Houston it was ten in the morning. The workday, geared to the East Coast financial market, had been in full swing for two hours. The receptionist was new on the job. She was wondering whether her blouse was too revealing for the staid image her employer was trying so hard to project. She looked down to inspect its neckline. Still, she thought, the younger men seemed to like it.

She wasn't sure what they did here. She had been told at the interview that it was a law firm, but so far she hadn't seen any evidence of criminals, cops, judges, private eyes. It wasn't at all like her favorite shows. No handcuffs, no pistols tagged as evidence. And so she was pleased when, through the glass doors that led to the elevators, walked four men, two in the uniform of the Harris County sheriff's office. They came to her marble-topped counter and stopped.

"May I help you?"

"How many exits are there to this floor?"

"I beg your pardon?"

One of the men in plainclothes repeated his question and she answered it. The deputies left.

The man in the dark suit spoke again.

"Does Roger Weedman work here?"

"Yes, he does." She was surprised. He seemed like a nice

man. The speaker showed her a badge and an identification card.

"Please call him to the reception desk. Tell him a Detective Lewis from Houston PD wants a word with him."

20

 By the start of the third month, November, Spector had harvested all the strawberries and asparagus. He had finished the works of Robert Louis Stevenson. He had entered so many transactions on the books of Spector Peripherals that the company could qualify for a listing on the New York Stock Exchange. He had dined at every good restaurant in the area once, the special places several times. At the best, Crissier, he was a regular. And almost every night he drove to Montreux to take his evening walks along the lakefront and listen for the complaining American twang he had come to recognize as his countryman's voice abroad.

Not that he was critical. Living overseas made him feel like an interloper. It wasn't the Swiss, who looked upon him as another eccentric from a land where wealth and oddity seemed wedded. It was his forced exile, his inability to breach the gap, to find a suitable tennis partner, bed partner. He'd settle for a dinner partner.

Now on the promenade evening came early, and fewer people walked when the cold wind came off the water. It would be better, Spector decided, looking at the lobby of one of the great hotels that stood across from him, it would be better to be inside.

He adopted the bar at the Palace Hotel as his refuge. Every evening he would arrive at seven, chat amiably with Alfred, the bartender, about the day's news, and drink Irish whiskey and soda, no ice. Two drinks, rarely a third, a discussion of NATO politics—he found the Americans inept and the Germans untrustworthy—then dinner in the hotel's dining room or one of the restaurants within walking distance. Winter slid down from the north, and lately, even when the wind came from the south, one could feel the chill of the Alps—Chablais, the Voiron, and Mont Blanc. And so the radius of his strolls grew shorter and shorter, and Spector, or, rather, Cyrus Reade, joined the regular clientele at the Palace.

On one of these evenings Spector sat with his first drink, considering where to walk, where to dine. It was his custom to sit at the far end of the bar, commanding a view of the room and allowing any others who chose a stool rather than a table their pick of seats. Most, he had observed, traveled in couples, and it was rare for there to be others with whom Spector shared Alfred's company.

This evening a large, well-dressed American entered, asked for a Jack Daniel's on the rocks, and sat expectantly cracking his knuckles as he waited for his glass. When it came, he watched it for a moment as if it might transmogrify, might spring to life and scurry away. This failing, he grabbed it in a huge hand and drank it off. He nodded to Alfred, who emptied the ice, made a new drink, and served it with a fresh napkin.

The customer looked around and settled on Spector.

"You speak English?" he asked.

"A little," Spector said with a grin.

"God. Glad to hear it. You learn the French word for 'another,' and as soon as you do, you're in some damn place where they speak something else. This is some damn country."

"It certainly is."

"You an American?" he said, brightening.

"Canadian," Spector answered. The man was set back, but only for a moment.

"What brings you here?" he asked.

"This hotel? Montreux?"

"Switzerland."

"Business."

"Oh," the man said, satisfied.

"Me," he went on, "my wife brings me. We're going to live four months abroad, she says. I don't know why I go along. We're usually in Jamaica by now. 'Course, they're all Sambos, and they'd slit your throat if they had the chance. But at least they speak English."

Without his support, Spector thought, the conversation would end. Instead the man was coming over to him, introducing himself, buying the next round. His name was Christopher Humphrey, but everyone called him Kit. The nickname, which Spector associated with youth, could not have been less suited. Kit Humphrey was, Spector guessed, just passing his mid-forties. He was a large man, six feet and wide. His girth was draped in well-tailored clothes, but still the stomach pushed against the shirt and the jacket fit snugly under the arms so the cuffs showed irregularly at the wrist. He wheezed slightly as he spoke. His face was lined and intense, but his eyes were dull, their fleshy lids seeming to have a will to close, and the resulting look was saturnine and scornful.

They say a man left adrift on the ocean will eat a seagull if he can catch it. Spector's desperation for company was severe, and he rarely cut off the random bar conversation. But his tolerance stopped short of Kit Humphrey. The man was intent on showing his worldliness by slurs, his sophistication by commonness. Spector was about to take his leave when Mrs. Humphrey walked in.

An elegant blond woman in a blue silk dress came through the smoked-glass door of the bar. At least as tall as Humphrey, slender, straw-colored hair to her shoulders. A thin, aniline complexion, lips slightly puffed and painted a hot pink, and blue eyes you could swim in. Spector had a habit of staring at beauty, and his habit had hold of him now.

"C'mere, honey. I want you to meet someone." It was unnecessary. She had come to his side and stopped.

"I've forgotten your name," Humphrey said.

"Reade. Cy Reade. Excuse my staring."

"I'm Devon Humphrey. And you're excused."

"We've been talking about home," Kit said. He drained the last drops from his glass.

"Will you join us for dinner, Cy?"

Spector had made vague reference to an appointment, so that he could gracefully refuse any invitation. Now he guessed, correctly, that Kit would have been paying no attention.

"If I'm not intruding," he said. He had adopted a courtly manner. After all, no one really knows how Canadians behave.

Spector enjoyed himself that evening. Humphrey continued to grouse, first about the confusing currency, then the prices, the weather. The hotel's kitchen was unnotable, and so Spector ordered simply: a grilled trout fillet with a watercress salad. He ordered the wine for all, and chose a white Epesses from a vineyard less than an hour's drive from where they sat. Humphrey continued to drink whiskey throughout the meal. but he seemed to hold it well, and neither his speech nor his mood changed.

The Humphreys were from Saint Louis. They had come to deliver their daughter, one of two, to start a year of high school in Lausanne. Their second was at boarding school in Connecticut. Devon spoke of them wistfully, as if they had died. Once on the Continent, she had convinced her husband to stay, to visit Paris, which he detested, and Rome, which he found full of foreigners. And now, since it was close to winter holidays, they had determined to stay in Switzerland, living in hotels, to visit their daughter on weekends, and to take her back to Saint Louis for Christmas.

As her husband was morose, Devon Humphrey was optimistic and giving. She asked questions to allow Spector-Reade to show himself to advantage, and she accepted his reticence on matters Canadian—Prime Minister Mulroney, the balance of trade, and the doings of Margaret Trudeau—as a gentlemanly disinclination to discuss politics and scandal at dinner. Or so Spector hoped, for he did not want to be seen as ignorant, particularly when he was.

Over dessert, Kit told them about the favorable Swiss tax structure. He had thought he'd come on a windfall—just stay in Switzerland. But, damn it, his accountant had assured him he still had to file a U.S. return.

"You can't imagine how unhappy Kit is with the taxes we have to pay," Devon said.

"I'd give an arm to beat the government out of a little. It's not only the money. It's what they use it for. They sweeten up

127

the welfare rolls so that every bum who can't speak English decides he's better off in the U.S. 'Course, you have your share too."

"I beg your pardon?"

"Those separatists. Don't you have those separatists?"

"Yes, we do. A free Quebec. But they've been quiet lately."

"Every country has them. Dissatisfied. Don't like their lot. Want to take away what you have and dole it out to everyone."

"The separatists." Spector was on thin ground. His spare knowledge came from an occasional magazine story. "The separatists don't want to share. They want to do the opposite. They want to keep me out."

"Amounts to the same thing. Whiners. Don't contribute, just criticize. We have 'em by the boatland. The spooks, the Mexicans. Give 'em something for nothing and it's not enough. That's another thing you have to admire about this country," Kit said. "Everybody works, and everybody gets along. No complaining."

"It took about four hundred years," Spector said amiably. "By now it seems to work fairly well." In five minutes he gave them what little he had learned of Swiss history, all from his readings in his small house on the hill. The drawing together of the bits of kingdoms for defense against the Hapsburgs, the early leagues, the civil wars, the wars of Burgundy, the wars of Milan, the wars of the Reformation, of Bohemia, of Willmargen. By the time they had reached the eighteenth century, Humphrey needed a brandy. Spector was safe on events of centuries ago. Having found a subject that did not incriminate him, he had gone on too long.

"I'm sorry," he said. "I seem to be lecturing." Kit grunted as if to accept the apology. Devon touched his sleeve for a second.

"I'd like to hear more," she said.

The bill came and Humphrey insisted on picking it up.

"That means you must allow me to reciprocate," Spector said, helping Devon with her chair.

"Then we'll be fortunate," Devon said with grace. "We'll have a return on our investment. Isn't that what businessmen are after?"

"That's right," her husband said, lighting a cigar. "We get two meals for one. A bad bargain you struck, Reade."

"I disagree," Spector said. He had not before had to play

the role of Cyrus Reade, and he was discovering in improvisation that it grew to his liking.

He said good night to the Humphreys in the lobby, and they agreed to meet the next day. He had seen the sights of the region and would be happy to show them what he most enjoyed.

"I'm not much of a museum man," Kit said.

Spector promised no museums, and left them to their own company.

His instincts had been refined for commercial liaisons rather than for emotional ones. Nonetheless, he understood that Devon Humphrey wanted his friendship. Whether she wanted more from him, he could not tell. She was a striking and vulnerable woman, and as is so often the case with extraordinary people, each quality enhanced the other.

The alloy captivated Spector, and he wanted to see more of her. But he knew from the start that any relationship would be temporary, that he had not recovered from three days with Cynthia. Nor did he seek recovery. She was in his thoughts daily. He wondered whether she had suffered at the bank because of him, whether she condemned or forgave him, whether, worse, she thought of him at all.

Now he steered his Citroën up the long drive to his mountain house with her ghost as a passenger. There was always the telephone. He carried the number of Empire State in his memory, and he could have her voice in minutes. She would be just finishing up at work. It was part of American folklore that many a perfect crime has been ruined because the looter couldn't sit still. So far he hadn't done anything to give himself away.

He poured himself an Irish whiskey, neat, and sat at the bay window, looking at the specks of light on the southern shore. Then he picked up the receiver and hit some numbers. What a wonderful invention.

"Lauren Henderson."

"Lauren?" The connection was clear.

"Yes?"

"I'm calling to see whether you want to play in the French Open with me. I thought we'd enter the women's and play in drag."

"Son of a bitch. Spector. Where the hell are you?"

"Europe, man. The land of Lendl and Borg."

"Hey, what'cha doing?"

"Nothing much. Working on a couple ideas. I just got homesick and decided you were the only person I could call."

"Hey. You're hard up. Got any news?"

"Only that I may have something for us. Hope to be back in a month or so."

"Out of sight. I'm looking at something too. If you meant what you said."

"Absolutely."

"This is a sweet deal. It's not ready yet. When it is, though, it's bigger than we talked. Maybe twice as big. Take, maybe, two million dollars. Maybe a little less."

"No problem. If it's a good deal, we can raise the money. I used to do that for a living, remember."

"Well, okay. I just don't think in those numbers."

He asked about his mail, and Lauren said the usual junk, nothing of interest, except a big package from London. Addressed to a company.

"Spector Peripherals?"

"That's it."

That would be the incorporation papers from the London solicitor. Papers to show the company in existence, all ordinary shares issued to Spector. Remarkable, he thought, our confidence in records. Where would I be without it?

Spector asked that Lauren do another favor and forward that package on. He gave him a post-office box number in Geneva.

"Hey, look. I got to run. I just wanted to hear your voice. I'll be in touch."

"Do, man, do. Like the ad says, reach out and touch someone."

"I keep saying that to the Swiss ladies, but so far no go."

Lauren laughed. He had a great laugh, Spector thought. Cleansing. They said goodbye.

Was that stupid? Mentioning Switzerland? You did fine until then. Still, there was nothing to connect the disappearing Roger Weedman to Spector. Hell, even if someone were looking for Spector, they couldn't connect him to Lauren unless they were fans of Saturday-morning tennis in Central Park. And that was a small crowd.

Spector's decision not to call Cynthia Olive was particularly fortuitous, though, had he phoned, Cynthia's companions that afternoon in New York would have been eager to speak to him. She sat, as Spector and Lauren spoke across the sea, in the office of a man named Korn, president of Empire State. With them were Tony Urso, two detectives from the city fraud unit, and a Mr. Gellhorn. If Gellhorn had a first name, no one had heard it. He alone looked dyspeptic, and indeed it was his company, Atlantic Fidelity, which bonded the bank for fraud, and which stood to take a $1.7-million loss. Minus the closing fees.

"The importance of this case," Gellhorn was saying, "can't be overemphasized. I am prepared to put all our resources on it. We won't allow someone to walk away with this money." He looked around for agreement.

"Now, the perpetrator has screwed up somewhere along the line. All we have to do is find out where. Right?"

In the silence, Mr. Korn said, Right. Urso and Cynthia Olive nodded unsurely. The two detectives waited quietly for him to finish.

"As the chief investigator for Atlantic Fidelity, my job is to recover that money. Your job," to the bank people, looking at them individually, "is to render all reasonable assistance. That's what the policy says. Your failure to render all reasonable assistance, I needn't remind you, could result in our taking the position that this loss isn't covered."

"You needn't remind us," said Mr. Korn.

Gellhorn wore glasses with dark tortoiseshell rims. They were improperly fitted, and he regularly tapped them back on his nose.

"Their job," waving in the direction of the two detectives, "is to take the facts I'll develop and find this impostor. Simple. If everyone does his job, we'll have this man locked up in no time."

"We're here to cooperate," said Korn.

"That's the way it'll work," Gellhorn said. "One, two, three. Like a good baseball infield. Are you a baseball fan, Miss Olive?"

"No, I'm not."

"Like a good baseball team. Surely you watch the World Series."

"Sorry," she answered.

"It's a matter of teamwork. Assuming," Gellhorn said ominously, "we're not sabotaged."

"What do you mean?" Korn asked him.

"This was a slick piece of work. Someone either knows a lot about banks or a lot about this bank."

The detectives stirred in their seats. Korn spoke directly.

"Mr. Gellhorn. I don't want you to cut short any investigations you think necessary. But I can save you some time. Tony Urso and Cynthia Olive are honest people. They're two of the best in our system. They're not involved in this."

"No one is beyond suspicion," Gellhorn said. "That is the way I work."

Korn agreed to make appointments for the investigators to interview six or seven people in the bank. The meeting was over.

The detectives and the man from Atlantic Fidelity went down in the elevator together. One of the cops had had his detective's badge for ten years, the other for twelve. Each was running more than a dozen cases. Primary responsibility. Crack shops, breaking and entering, a rapist who specialized in women over seventy. One mugger rolled bums in the park for their shoes, then stuck a screwdriver in their eyes. Gellhorn's case was about money. The man who took it was long since gone. The lost dough would be recovered by the bonding company in premiums. It might take them six months. Maybe longer.

"Look, Mr. Gellhorn. Here's my card. You get hold of something, you let us know."

"I'm on it, Lieutenant. I'll be in touch."

"Yeah. Do that."

The cops got in their unmarked Plymouth, double-parked on Broadway.

"How do you like Dick Tracy?" one said.

The other started up the car and pulled out into the traffic before answering.

"What an asshole."

21

Spector became their guide. Three or four times a week they met after lunch in the *fin-de-siècle* lobby of the Palace, and he announced their outing. If he had in mind a second destination, he assured the two were separated by a glass of wine. As a couple, the Humphreys seemed held together by their polarity. He enjoyed shopping, and would rarely leave a site, no matter how spiritual, without finding something to buy. She liked the moods of places, the castles, the cathedrals, and wanted to know why they were there. He had studied French in high school and refused to use it; she had no classroom learning, but she had picked up a phrase or two and always ordered in French, even when, as was usually the case, the waiter's English was perfect.

Spector enjoyed their company, and he had turned his mind to filling in their personalities, much as he used to decode crosswords. That of Kit Humphrey was easier. His great-grandfather had started a small grocery store in what was now part of downtown Saint Louis. By the time he died at ninety-one, he had assembled a chain, Kit didn't know how. Over one hundred stores in several states, as well as a wholesale fruit-and-vegetable business, a specialty importer, and a private brand of marmalades, jams, and baked beans.

After his death, his son, Kit's grandfather, sold the stores to a national supermarket chain in Cleveland, the private labels to Beatrice Foods, and the wholesale business to a local syndicate.

He had kept the importer for his own amusement. In his one business attempt, Kit's father had run the little company into bankruptcy. But the loss was insignificant compared with the family assets.

"Grandpa said when he sold out that five generations of his family would never have to work," Kit told them. "But the way this government keeps taking bites out of you, hell, it may not be true. It's the damn Internal Revenue. The progressive tax system is the greatest disincentive to productivity since Karl Marx."

She was a puzzle more difficult to solve. They told Spector that they had met while she was waiting tables at a lodge in Stowe. He was on a skiing holiday. She had been modeling in New York, hands and neck only, which Spector understood to mean that those were the parts of her body in demand. He examined them for their professional appeal.

She left the business, she said, because of the pressures, and Spector read in the slight flaring of her nostrils and deflected eyes her sturdy and offended modesty.

Devon was a fragile person. She had been born in upstate New York, of a shopkeeper and his wife. She had finished high school and gone directly to the city. When she was younger, she wanted to be a professional musician—she had studied the violin—but it had been a fantasy, not an ambition, or so she insisted, because she had no talent. Yes, she told him, she was enjoying Europe. Unlike Kit, she didn't miss cheeseburgers, "Dynasty," and shopping at supermarkets. She missed only her children.

"If we were home, I suppose, they would still be away at school."

Spector remarked that she was so young to have two teen-aged daughters, and she said they had had their children early.

"I don't want you to think there was any plan in all that," Kit said. "She makes it sound as if it was a good idea." And Devon again looked down to the table.

"She joins middle age next week," Kit said grandly. "Monday, Devon will be forty."

"We'll have to celebrate," said Spector. "Would you let me give a little party? Just for the three of us."

She smiled at him warmly. "That would be nice, Cy."

Why, he asked himself driving home that evening, had he

been so eager to host a dinner? For one thing, Humphrey leaped to get every check as if Spector couldn't possibly afford it.

For a second he felt Devon's need for care. Perhaps his solicitude could provide an emotional convalescence, however brief, to restore her. He felt that she was failing. Her thin complexion called to his mind the translucence of a butterfly, and a wounded butterfly does not easily regenerate herself.

Although she might welcome a young and affirmative lover, he was still wrapped up in the image of Cynthia Olive and the possibility that he might see her again. Whether that knowledge was the cause or the effect, he could not say, but there was something else about Devon, and it surprised him. He did not find her sexually appealing. Fascinating, yes, and beautiful. But not the object of his stalk. He was a hunter of quail coming upon a young bird, crippled and fluttering in the sage.

He would plan a party. It would be a special event, and he would include favorite foods and touches. For Kit, his whiskey—black-label Jack Daniel's poured with American club soda, not the effete European bottled water—his cigars—Monte Cristo number threes—and a meal he could pronounce. For her, caviar, ambience, a great champagne, and no talk about business. Poetry, history, art, and architecture.

Rather, almost no talk.

Spector had an idea. He would not have entertained it had he not found Kit Humphrey boorish, unappreciative, and unpatriotic. And had Lauren not mentioned the need for a second million. It would be nice to be able to do the deal without taking in any other partners to provide the second million. Unlike Humphrey, Spector did not begrudge Uncle Sam his share of Cy Reade's money. But, given the rate of exchange and the cost of the life Cy Reade had chosen, after U.S. taxes Spector would end up with a little over a million.

It was a hell of an idea. Spector promised himself to introduce it only if Humphrey persisted.

Which, of course, Humphrey always did.

The birthday dinner was a great success. Instead of the elegant restaurants of the town—the Pont de Brent or the two star François Doyen—Spector hired a car and driver and they set out for a short drive into the country to a transformed stable. The main dining room had a split-level floor, and they walked through the gathering crowd to their private table in the raised section. On the walls hung an assortment of rural decorations: lights in brass bells, the pelts and horns of chamois goats, farm tools. And every baluster, every rail had been carved to bring out the faces and curves hiding within.

Much of the carving and all of the atmosphere were the doing of the owner, who greeted Spector at the door and made a fuss about his party. This large, bearded man wore a leather shirt, a chef's cap, and knickers. He was delighted, he announced, to find that his best Canadian patron, the only Canuck he'd ever met who knew wines, had found not one friend but two.

The Roederer flowed; the *ris montagnard* and veal were eaten; Devon seemed to glow through her translucent skin.

It was the end of the meal. They sat, three of them watching the flame leap at the end of Kit's cigar.

"Now, you tell me," he said between puffs. "What's wrong with a country that has Cuban tobacco and low taxes?"

"They don't speak English," Spector guessed. He and Devon laughed.

"Right. Now all we have to do is combine the advantages of each."

Spector took a breath.

"I'm surprised, Kit, with all your access, you don't do something about those taxes."

"Do something? I'd hate to tell you what I pay every year for lawyers and accountants to save my money."

"They won't help. Not much. They use," and here Spector took what he thought a tantalizing pause, "the conventional ways."

Kit leaned forward.

"If I thought there was a way to pay less in taxes and not get caught, hell, I'd do it. I'd be a fool not to, isn't that right? That's what everybody does."

"Absolutely," Spector agreed.

"We don't pay too much," Devon said.

"Anything you don't have to is too much."

"Right," Kit agreed. "What do you do, Cy?"

"Well," Spector answered slyly, "let's just say I pay all my taxes. But let's say that somebody else I know has been hanging around Switzerland long enough to know what the big boys do."

136

Kit was hooked. He held his cigar in front of him, its smoke blocking his view. He moved it to get a better look and waved away the trails.

"Here you are in the heart of the best and most secret banking system in the world. Once you get money into a Swiss account, so long as there isn't probable cause of a felony, what happens in that account is only your business. Nobody else's. All you pay is transaction fees. Which, I should tell you, are quite reasonable. Once it's in the bank, you can buy stock on the exchanges, taxables, whatever you like, and no one need know what you're doing.

"The trouble with invested capital is that it leaves tracks. You can't put it somewhere to make money and not have it known about, because they've known about it for years. The first thing you have to do is lose some money."

"I don't follow," said Kit.

"You lose some money. Make an investment, it gets lost. You take a capital loss for tax purposes. And somehow that money turns up in a numbered account. *Voilà.*"

Kit looked at him. "That's it?"

"That's it."

"But doesn't the investment get audited? Don't they find you that way?"

"Your Internal Revenue has limited resources. It can certainly find out about a company you invest in in, say, Saint Louis. But what do they do if it's a Common Market company? Let's say, a United Kingdom company that's up and going?

"For example, I have several little service companies I use. Let's say you invest in one of them. Reade Holdings. You buy into its preference shares. Let's say that investment doesn't turn out. Instead, the single creditor comes and presents Reade Holdings with a demand to pay its debts. And the money you've invested is the only money Reade has available. Why, you lose everything, Reade Holdings goes bankrupt, and the creditor gets paid."

"And the creditor?"

"Turns out the creditor uses a numbered account somewhere abroad. Say, for example, Crédit Suisse in Geneva. And it turns out as well that this creditor is a friend of yours, and has provided that you are the signatory on the account."

Humphrey seemed mesmerized. Spector heard only his

phthistic breathing. Devon and he remained silent, listening to that whisper. Kit did not like business, but he liked business schemes. Spector thought again of the plateau. Don't pull too hard.

"Enough talk of commerce," Spector said. Humphrey shook his head as if awakening.

"Now, Kit, instead of your usual brandy, I want you to try this." The owner came forward with a bottle of white wine in a towel. The frost on the bottle suggested a recent but mild chill. The interruption stopped conversation, and although Humphrey wanted it to go on, Spector had mastered the situation, and his guests both watched him as if he were a magician.

"I've chosen this Sauternes especially because I know that you both will like its taste, and Devon especially its romance. Like her it is blonde, complicated, and majestic, and the years make it, as they do her, only more so." Three glasses were poured.

Spector lifted his. "Happy birthday," he said, and he wished in that instant that he were married and, if he could not be married to Cynthia, that he were married to her.

The wine, Château d'Yquem, had a particular flavor. It was strong and fresh as cream, but it had no richness afterwards, no coating of the mouth, so that as you drank it you wanted more.

Devon agreed. Taste was so hard to describe. "Like love," she said, then added quickly, "or music. It *is* like cream, and cream always reminds me of Chopin. I don't know why."

While they sat, Devon asked him to tell the romance he had promised. And he told them of the fairy-book castle that is the château at Yquem, sitting atop a hill, at which all the machinery, without exception, is made of wood. There the steps of wine-making are observed like a medieval order, the product not released until it has the inspection and care attending a Rolls. And he told them the story of the neighboring vineyard, at Rayne-Vigneau, where in 1925 the most remarkable event occurred.

"The owner was a renowned scholar and a talented water-colorist. He was a French nobleman, a man of the highest repute. One season, to his surprise, as laborers were working the earth, precious stones began turning up in the vineyard. Newspaper people came from all over. Uncut stones from sources around the world were found. The owner swore he had no idea how they had appeared there, and indeed he would have no reason to lie. There are still two thousand in the family's collection. They say more than twelve thousand stones were found. Fire-red cornelians and opals from Hungary, sapphires, jasper, onyx, and Madagascar amethysts. No one could explain how they got there, and to this day the riddle is unsolved."

The effect was riveting. Humphrey's cigar burned down toward his knuckle. Devon watched him intently, her lips slightly parted, the width of a pea pod. He could make away with her and be back before Humphrey realized, but for the smoking of that elegant fuse. Spector was not sure which of them he was seducing.

The last of the Sauternes was poured. Devon, not a drinker, had had only one glass. The rest he and Kit put away, and Spector felt sure that Kit neither needed nor wanted his help for the task.

They returned to the Palace, where Spector had left his car. Devon kissed him lightly on the cheek and thanked him for the best birthday gift ever. Kit shook his hand firmly.

"Listen, Cy. About that tax scheme. You really think that could be done?"

He put his left hand on Kit's bicep and shook again. The man had wide, flabby arms.

"Better than that. It *has* been done. A dozen times. Good night, old man. We'll talk later."

"Yes, later. And thanks for a wonderful evening."

"I've asked for this conference," Gellhorn said, "because we're not getting anywhere. The police have run down the Mexican bank numbers, the post-office boxes, the phone logs from the Parishes' house. I've spoken to everyone who met the suspect. I've been to Lake Forest twice. I've even found the waiter who served the breakfast at the Pierre."

He paused and studied Cynthia ominously.

"I'm convinced we're missing something.

"Or, to put it more plainly, that we're not getting everything."

Cynthia came at him.

"Just a minute, Mr. Gellhorn. If you're saying I'm involved in this, then say so. I've spoken with you, with the gentlemen from the police, with the FBI, as often as you want. I've gone over this story with you a dozen times. You want to make a charge, make it." You learn how to confront authority early on Lenox Avenue. It's not by taking the first step back.

"Now, Miss Olive. That's not what I'm saying. You and Mr. Urso here"—Urso imperceptibly slunk down in his chair—"have given us all the time we've asked for. That's true." He nodded to Mr. Korn to communicate his approbation, and with his middle finger pushed his glasses back on his nose.

"We want you to make sure you haven't missed anything, that's all. Any little piece, what he said, what he wore, where he said he was going. Other than Hong Kong."

"You checked that out?" Urso asked. One of the New York cops answered.

"Nothing. Of course, he would be traveling on his own passport, and we don't know his name. But we've checked the list of single Americans departing for Hong Kong in the ten days after the closing and we've come up with nothing. *Nada*."

"Someone in Chicago?"

Gellhorn took a small memo pad from his back pocket and flipped through its pages.

"The gardener saw him drive out a few times. Never spoke to him. None of the neighbors added anything. Mr. and Mrs. . . ." He looked for their names. ". . . Kittredge live closest. They were aware of him, or she was. But she didn't see enough of him to get an impression."

Gellhorn looked at the assembled group smugly. Then he went on.

"Atlantic Fidelity stands to take a major loss here. I want you to realize that. And we want to be satisfied that our insured and its employees have done everything they could to help us out. That's a condition of the policy. If we're not convinced, we don't have to pay."

Korn spoke up.

"Anything you want us to do, we're ready to do."

"I can't tell you what you haven't remembered. That's all." Gellhorn continued to look at Cynthia. He was applying interrogation techniques. "I just want the bank and you to realize your obligations."

Cynthia heard the subliminal message. Gellhorn was troubled that a bank he covered had a Puerto Rican loan officer, born in Harlem. He had said as much to Korn after he had seen her personnel file. She felt temper straining around her brow, but she kept her composure.

"Mr. Gellhorn, Tony and I will go over it once again. Maybe one of us can trigger something the other forgot. If we do, we'll let you know."

"I would appreciate that, Cynthia. I'm glad to see you realize the seriousness of this matter. My company doesn't take these losses easily."

"Yeah. Well, you know," she said dreamily as she stood up to leave, "maybe you ought to get them to lighten up."

Urso ran after her in the hall.

"We really going to do that, Cynthia? I mean, you want to go over this again?"

"Are you kidding me? Man, if there was anything else, we'd have thought of it by now. He can take a flying leap."

"Right," said Tony, eager to agree. "He's a pain in the ass. I don't like his attitude."

It's not Gellhorn's attitude, she thought. It's Gellhorn. What are you doing working in a bank, kid? Why aren't you uptown, working on your back or standing on the ADC line? He can take a flying leap.

Sure, she remembered some little things. Every night since he left. The mole on his shoulder. The roughness of one of his hands. She had felt it with her palm, her lips, her breast. When she asked him about the calluses on the heel of his right hand, he said that's where he held a racquet. The waiter at that restaurant who had known him by another name. Those things might be helpful.

She returned to her desk and opened the center drawer. She had marked up the classifieds from the Sunday *Times* and circled in black the only four ads for bankers. It looked like slim pickings.

22

The celebration was what he had hoped. That next morning Spector suffered from the immoderate amount of wine he had consumed. He awoke early, anxious and dissatisfied, put on a sweat suit and sneakers, and forced himself to run four miles over the hilly roads outside Vevey. After a damp October, the late fall had been moderate and clear, and as he ran he had glimpses of the gray-green lake below.

What will six months away do to my game? he wondered. Probably what it has done to my sex glands. My serve will recede into memory. And then he thought of Cynthia, and of whether there were not some other invention he could conceive which would allow him to reappear as Edgar Parish, claim her, and take her away. Here, perhaps.

He returned to his little house, sprinting from the bicycle shed up the hill. As he entered, gasping in pain and contrition from the penance he had done, the telephone was ringing. It was only eight-thirty.

"Hello. Did I wake you?" It was Kit Humphrey.

"No, I've been up and out."

"You said you were an early riser. Look, I've been thinking. How quickly do you suppose we could do that? I could use the loss for this year, and if you really meant that about using one of your companies . . ."

"Yes. I think we could do it fast. You'd have to decide on an amount. The rest my solicitors will handle."

"They're reliable?"

"Cream of the crop."

"What do you think about an amount?"

"Well," Spector said judiciously, "the first time you do this, you want to pick the right number. Not too small to make it not worth your while, but not so much you get greedy. Don't want your Revenue boys thinking the horses have been stolen from the barn. Say," and here he seemed to consider amounts like tomatoes in a bin, "one million U.S."

"Good," said Humphrey. "One million. Round sum. What do we do next?"

"Let me think," Spector answered. As he did so, he opened the table drawer and withdrew a yellow legal tablet on which he had written out every step.

"First you open an account. Crédit Suisse, Geneva. Or, if you like, I'll open it for you. You'll have to sign signature cards and provide a passport number."

"No, you do all that. I'll sign the cards. Just me on the signature, I think."

"Right. Next I'll have my lawyers do up the boiler plate. Usual stuff, telling you what you're investing in. Once the papers are ready, you have the money wired to the solicitors. That gives the whole thing the stamp of authority. You'll get a closing binder, stock certificates, prospectus."

"Great. What'll this whole thing cost me? The lawyers have fees for all this, don't they?"

"Don't worry about it. Your money will sit in their account for a couple of days. The interest will cover it."

"I can't tell you how much this means to me, Reade. This is great of you."

"Don't mention it. Happy to oblige."

Spector did ten minutes of calisthenics before his shower. Bicycles, push-ups, sit-ups. Getting flabby. *All I have to do is run like that every day and increase my exercises by, say, ten percent a week. I'll be back in fighting shape.*

He showered, shaved, dressed in business suit, and went off for the day. Geneva was an easy drive, although, having no business there, he had rarely made it since coming the other way, light years ago, out of Dulles Airport.

First he visited his post box, taken in his real name. His only mail was from Lauren, and indeed only Lauren had this mailing address. The packet included some bills that he had overlooked and that would now have to go without payment for a while. But the single largest envelope was the one he had asked for. In it, the London solicitor, a John Millington, had forwarded the papers to complete his new corporation, Spector Peripherals. There were articles of association for a private limited-liability company, several lengthy subscription agreements, and—he supposed for the studious—a copy of the Companies Act of 1985. He need only fill in the blanks and send it back. Mr. Millington had also included his firm's statement for services: £350.

Spector checked his watch. Too early to call New York. His next stop was his bank. By design, he had never visited it before. All his transactions had been by telephone and mail.

There he merely picked up two applications for numbered accounts. He asked the clerk if, by any chance, they could have sequential numbers, and she assured him that was possible. If he would merely tell her the names of the accounts, she could hold two account numbers for twenty days.

That would be fine, he said. An individual account for Christopher Humphrey and a corporate account for Reade Holdings, Ltd. Reade with an "e."

A light lunch, some shopping, and the leisurely drive back to Vevey.

The house he had rented was furnished in an eclectic way. Leather and upholstered furniture from no discernible period, one or two Chinese rugs of quality, and several machine-loomed imitations. All in all, though, it was a comfortable setting. And it was complete. Corkscrews, pliers, cocktail napkins, extra fuses. It had everything. And in the drawer of a desk in the corner, an ancient Hermes typewriter.

Spector picked the dead leaves off his house plants and watered the scented geraniums that lined the large bay window in the central room. Then he took out the Hermes and typed the following letter:

John Millington, Esq.
Mason and Sample
128 Newgate
London EC4,
England

Dear Mr. Millington,

I have your name from my New York lawyers. I am a Canadian citizen living in Switzerland. I should like to start a new venture, using a U.K. corporation, and I ask that you take the necessary steps in getting it underway.

The new venture is to be called Reade Holdings, Ltd. I will be in partnership with an American, Christopher Humphrey. Each shall contribute $1 million, U.S., to commence operations. The purpose of the venture will be to acquire companies in the computer field.

For my contribution, I shall receive a senior debenture of $1 million (U.S.) and shall be the company's sole creditor. Mr. Humphrey shall be issued 10,000 shares of preference stock, $100 par value, with a 5% cumulative dividend and mandatory redemption in six years. He and I shall then divide the common stock equally.

Although Mr. Humphrey and I are friends of long standing, for our own protection I would like you to prepare a short prospectus explaining the risks of this investment to him. I want there to be no question that he understands the relative position of creditor and senior security holder, so that if the company does not go as we planned, the fact that my debt gets paid before his preferred shares does not come as a surprise to him.

I shall be the only officer of the company, and shall be solely authorized to withdraw its funds. I have listed all the other information on the enclosure. I hope you have sufficient information to get started. We hope to have a closing shortly. Prior to closing, both Mr. Humphrey and I will wire the required funds to your account. Incidentally, I enclose a bank draft for £350 as an advance for your fees.

Business calls me to Belgium much of the near future, but either Kit Humphrey or I will be in touch with you.

Yours faithfully,
Cyrus MacNeil Reade

On the promised enclosure he listed Reade's date and place of birth, mailing address, passport number, bank reference. He would have to get the same information from Humphrey and insert it, but he had no doubts of Kit's eagerness to cooperate.

At last the earth had spun enough so that New Yorkers were rousing and getting on with the day. One thing about a flat-earth theory, Spector mused. It would make transatlantic business more convenient.

The lawyer had not arrived at his Wall Street office yet, but his secretary could take the message. Spector gave her all the missing ingredients for Spector Peripherals, all the questions Millington had asked. He explained that he'd like it relayed because he was traveling and found it difficult to get hold of his English solicitors.

"Lawyers all over the world are the same, aren't they? Elusive. Slippery."

The secretary laughed and agreed.

One more thing. Moneys might be coming in for Spector Peripherals. Spector hoped he could have those wired and held in their firm's trust account. The secretary said of course, they did that all the time.

After he rang off, he reflected on his lines of defense. First of all, Humphrey would have no legal grounds to complain. The money he invested would go exactly where he had agreed it would go, to purchase preference shares in a risky venture. Would he instead have the temerity to say, No, it was supposed to go to me? It was supposed to defraud the IRS. Unlikely he would raise that cry. If he did, he would have to explain away the prospectus, with all its predictions of ruin and failure. And if he were able to explain it away, he would still have to find Cyrus Reade, who would by then have joined the revenant ranks of Roger Weedman and Edgar Parish.

Spector posted the letter by express mail. He knew the Humphreys were staying in Europe only until their daughter was released for the Christmas recess, and then it was back to Saint Louis. He needed to have this wrapped up before they left.

"Cynthia?"

"Yes," she said expectantly. It had been a long time since she had heard that voice, and it had faded from her recall.

"You're a tough lady to find."

146

"Who is this?" After a moment's doubt she knew it wasn't he, and her voice regained its edge.

"Gellhorn. Atlantic Fidelity. You're a tough lady to find," he said again.

"I'm a tough lady. What can I do for you, Mr. Gellhorn?"

"Why did you change to a delisted number?"

"Single woman gets her name in the paper, gets a lot of calls from creeps. Looks like I'm still not immune."

"You like to give people a hard time." No response.

"I just wanted to let you know, Cynthia." That first-name crap got to her too. "The police are dropping this investigation. Not closing it, but they have no place to go. But we're not. We're keeping our eye on you and Urso. Both with new jobs, you with an unlisted number. We're keeping our eye on you."

"Mr. Gellhorn?"

"Yes?"

"Fuck off." She hung up the phone.

23

The pace was picking up. Spector no longer had time for the leisurely bike rides, and the calisthenics he would have to resume when he got back to the States. Besides, what he needed was a second serve that spun off sharply, not a well-defined physique.

What was it Mozart had written about an aria? It was in *Così fan Tutte.* He had marked it *presto,* but in his letters said that the tenor should sing it in practice as fast as he could, and then perform it faster.

He had been at rest too long. He was ready for a little pace, the lists of things to do, the planning.

Kit Humphrey was most accommodating. He performed on schedule the tasks Spector assigned to him. The signature cards and information for the account at Crédit Suisse came back the next day. So did the missing data Spector needed for the law firm. Humphrey told him his Saint Louis firm had checked on Mason and Sample and confirmed that they were first-rate. Kit had also assembled a million dollars plus transfer fees in a local bank in cash equivalents, ready for wiring upon notice.

Establishing telephone contact between Switzerland and Panama City was nettlesome. Eventually Spector got through. Señor Guitterez was ready to be of service. All moneys sent from Crédit Suisse to the United States would be passed through the Panamanian accounts, their own Ellis Island.

Then there was Lauren.

"Spector, I can't believe you."

"What do you mean?"

"You're out of here three, four months, you come back with two million bucks. What do you do, wire your body with plastique?"

"Do you want to know?"

Lauren laughed, that cathartic laugh that left nothing behind.

"No, man. I don't want to know."

"Can you get them to stand still until January?"

"No problem. I know I can do that."

"Send me their numbers. I want to study the deal before we plunk the money down."

"I hope to hell. Same P.O. box?"

"Yeah. Geneva. Then I'll take what you send me, go somewhere warm, and read through the New Year, and be in town for a mid-month closing if it all looks kosher."

"It looks it to me. But, then, who's Jewish?"

"How's your game?"

148

"You gotta come back. The only guys I know can beat me. I'm getting depressed."

"Be in touch."

He called the bank in Geneva. Yes, Mr. Reade, the two accounts had been established. All paper was in order. Before Mr. Humphrey could withdraw, he would have to come in and establish his identity. No, he could deposit without that. And, no, that would not be necessary for Mr. Reade, since he was an established customer of the bank.

The clerk could send Mr. Reade's deposit book to him, but she would have to send the other book directly to Mr. Humphrey. At the Palace in Montreux. Would that be sufficient?

Yes, it would be, so long as he could have both numbers for his file.

She thought that would be permissible. After all, Mr. Reade had brought Mr. Humphrey to them. The numbers were sequential. Spector jotted them down as she spoke:

Humphrey   102 LE 2749
Reade Holdings 102 LE 2750

That was fine, he said. No, he assured her, he would not get them confused.

And the following day brought the documents from Millington. They were accompanied by a prolix and tedious letter, urging Reade to call him, as his firm did not like to transact business without knowing its clients. Millington had enclosed the prospectus, form of debenture, description of the preferred shares, and an affirmation to be signed by Humphrey. All in order.

It was set. One last step. Schedule the closing. This was a Thursday. Monday wasn't too early. He would get Humphrey to sign these documents tonight, wire the funds tomorrow. London would keep them over the weekend. He would fly into Gatwick Monday morning, back Monday night and out.

If only that schedule comported with Mr. Millington's.

It did.

"Then that will be satisfactory," he asked. "Two o'clock on Monday at your offices?"

"It will, Mr. Humphrey. It will indeed. Though I must say, I would prefer if Mr. Reade could also attend."

"He sends his regrets, Mr. Millington. He called as soon as he got your package and asked me to handle it. We're old friends, and we've done several deals together. He has to be in Brussels these next days."

"He'd mentioned that in his letter. Your bank has called also, to get our international wiring account."

"Well, it sounds as if it's all in order, then."

"I suppose so. I would feel more comfortable if you were both to be here, but I suppose we can proceed."

"Excellent. See you Monday, then."

"Yes. Oh, one last thing."

"Yes?"

"I needn't mention it, because you'll have it with you. Your passport."

"Excuse me."

"Your passport. We'll need you to verify your identification with it. But of course you'll be carrying it with you to leave and re-enter Switzerland."

"Of course."

"See you then."

"Oh, Mr. Millington."

"Yes?"

"I just remembered. I promised to take my wife somewhere on Monday. Would Tuesday, same time, be all right?"

"Let me check. Yes, I think so."

"Good. Let's call it Tuesday."

"Goodbye, then."

"Goodbye."

Spector hung up, stunned. It was one matter to walk into a room where everyone was expecting Humphrey, using the voice they knew as Humphrey's, and announce that you were he. It was quite another to produce a passport confirming that identity. Clearly he couldn't count on luring Kit into the stall of a men's room.

He had but one thought. It lacked finesse, it lacked certitude, originality. Indeed, Spector realized to his chagrin, it was a bit of a cliché.

The extra day he had sought was not merely to delay for

time. The bars at the hotel were always closed on Sunday nights. He would need their help.

The three friends were returning from an Alpine outing. They had taken Spector's Citroën on a clear November day on the road north of Montreux, climbing steeply past the summer spas, into the snows. At the end of the road they took a cog railway to Rochers de Naye, not yet open for skiing but without season on its breathtaking views. It was a scramble from there to the peak's summit at over two thousand meters. They lunched in a surprisingly warm sun on the patio of a charming hotel near the peak. But Kit was too excited to eat. And, coming back in the car, he went over the details of the scheme.

"Wonderful. All I do, then, is call my bank." He looked at his watch. "They'll open in two hours. They wire the funds to the Limey lawyers, the lawyers do this hocus-pocus with the papers we signed, and put the money in my account here."

"Remember," Spector warned. "Not a word to the lawyers. They know nothing about the misdirection of funds. This is one of the oldest firms in London. They wouldn't have any part of this."

"Right. It's so simple. So brilliant. And we don't have to be there or anything?"

"Correct. In fact, I won't be around on Tuesday, when the money changes hands. I have to spend the day in Geneva. But the funds will show up at your account at Crédit Suisse, probably by the end of the week." He handed Kit the card showing his new account number.

Devon was somber. She was bored by talk of commerce, hadn't liked this plan since they began talking about it, and felt Reade had drifted from her in the process.

"Pity about Tuesday," Spector went on. "We really ought to celebrate Kit's emancipation from bondage. I was hoping we would mark the occasion."

"Emancipation. Right you are," Kit said happily. "We'll have dinner. When you get back."

"Afraid I can't do it then, and I may have to be traveling the end of that week." Then, brightening, "How about Monday night?"

"Sure," said Kit. "Monday would be fine."

151

"Tell you what. To make it a little different, we'll do it stag. You won't mind, will you, Devon? Two bachelors on the town. I promise to bring him home."

Spector knew that she would be hurt and that she would acquiesce. They had never excluded her before, not because of her husband's devotion to her but because Spector could not bear his company without hers.

"Where shall we go?" Kit's globed eyes put Spector in mind of a salamander.

"Leave that to me," he answered. "I'll make the arrangements. And I can promise you," he said with as close as he could manage to a leer, "no museums."

"No museums," Humphrey roared. What salacious pleasures he was imagining, Spector could not guess. Contemplation of the tax savings, the adventure of his one million dollars, and now this had him in a state of high agitation.

"Bachelors' night out," he said. "But this has to be on me. On me. I insist. And no museums."

24

Spector made the arrangements for the evening. Dinner reservations at the Casino Grille, a corner table. A call to the barman at the Palace for what he hoped would be the quietus, the final coup.

He telephoned Kit and arranged to meet at the Palace bar for a first drink.

"And bring your passport. I have to check something for the solicitors."

Humphrey agreed.

Alfred was happy to have them. The long season was under way, the respite between close of the music festival and the arrival of the first holiday tourists. In the bar were two Japanese drinking coffee, an elderly foursome from Lugano, and a young man in a jacket worn over a Wisconsin sweat shirt. Economic fortunes had relaxed the hotel's dress code. In better times Alfred would have sent the collegian packing.

Kit downed his first Jack Daniel's and ordered a second while Spector nursed a tall whiskey. That ratio might be enough. Spector struck up a conversation with the young American. He was from Eau Claire and had decided to take off a semester. He didn't much care for psychology, his major. But he didn't much care for Europe either. And beer was three times the price. He had heard Munich was fun, and that earlier there had been a bunch of kids there from the Big Ten.

Spector liked him: he was lonely, lost, vapid. He reminded Spector of himself. And not necessarily at college.

"Shit," said Humphrey, "when I was his age, I wasn't hanging around adults' bars. I was out looking for ass."

"Maybe he just looks in different places."

Spector considered the hazards of the evening. Most probable, and most benign, was that he would be unconscious by dessert. He could not stay even with Humphrey, a man whose capacity seemed the equal of his appetite.

A second, far uglier prospect was that Humphrey, whose sober company he didn't favor, would with drink turn lubricious and nasty. Spector had a vague hunch that Humphrey was bisexual. He had no basis for his feeling, other than his dislike of the man. At best it would be a long evening. If Humphrey had several unattractive traits, wasn't it logical to assume that over more time more unpleasantness would be revealed?

Their dinner at the Grille was satisfactory. No better. It took little skill to keep the conversation on those subjects which titillated rather than outraged Spector's companion. And, for his part, Kit was affable, pleasant. He flirted with the woman at the

153

cloakroom and with the aging frau who served the bread tray. Spector noted with relief that the rest of the service staff was male and distant.

They had another round of drinks at the table, and Spector assured they continued their two-to-one ratio. A claret with the meal, and afterwards a Cointreau each, and Kit a brandy. Unluckily, Kit declined any more, pointing out that Spector wasn't holding his own.

"I almost forgot." Spector delivered the line with mock alarm. "We have to stop off at your hotel bar for a nightcap."

"Not for me," Humphrey said. "I've probably had enough."

"Enough?" said Spector, as if offended by the word. "Humphrey, old man, let me paraphrase Mozart for you. Tonight we are going to drink as much as we can, and then we'll drink a little more."

They walked into the darkened bar at the Palace. Only one couple shared the room with them, at the far end, head to head in conversation.

"Alfred. Do you have that bottle of Y'Quem I've asked you to keep iced?"

"Yes, Mr. Reade."

"Uncork it, please, for me and my friend Mr. Humphrey. And ask the kitchen to send out a small plate of fruit and cheeses. Gorgonzola perhaps. A peach. And some Emmenthal."

Alfred nodded. The order was waiting in his refrigerator by the sink.

Two cut-glass goblets were placed on the bar between them, and the cheese tray set in the middle. In the reduced light, the crystal caught the beams from the recessed bulbs, diffused them, sent them out in shards. Spector felt heady from drink, and he suggested they move to a booth. Alfred assisted, waiting until they were settled before producing the bottle. He held it before them in a crisp white towel to show its label.

"I remember how much you enjoyed this Sauternes before, Kit. I thought it would be the perfect way to finish off our celebration."

If Humphrey had been anticipating a night of bachelor joys, he was now ready to compromise them for those of a more familiar thirst. He watched as Alfred carefully peeled the lead from the bottle's crown, wiped off a thin mauve residue with the clean linen cloth, and turned the simple screw into the cork.

154

Even the sound of its giving was filled with pleasure, a soft, pliant squeak, an animal consent.

Spector watched Humphrey watching Alfred. True, the waiter, as he had been asked, gave the event its full ritual. Humphrey was by now ten minutes from his last drink, and Spector sensed the pull that heightened his anticipation. The cork gave with a soft pop. Kit had removed a speck of tobacco from his mouth and had not withdrawn his tongue. Its tip showed, pink and salient. Finally Alfred poured a splash in Spector's glass.

"My friend," he said to Humphrey.

"Oh, no. You're the wine expert."

"I insist. Besides, this is the wine you so much enjoyed. You have become its final judge."

Humphrey could wait on ceremony no longer. As he looked on it, the wine shone gold, like autumn leaves when the sun lights them from behind. He put the taste to his lips, and with the greatest exercise of will sipped it between his lips.

"Extraordinary," he said softly. Then he said it again.

Alfred gave a shallow bow, poured each a glass, placed the bottle on the table, and withdrew.

They toasted each other silently, and took the wine. Kit finished his glass in a draught.

"Before I forget," Spector said. "Your passport."

Humphrey produced it from his breast pocket and Spector copied down data at random. He would discard the notepaper as soon as he got home. Humphrey took the opportunity to have a second glass of wine. He was delighted that Spector seemed more interested in the research and the cheeses, and took advantage of the unequal division of thirst, for although they sat before a full bottle, its contents would diminish, and a chance to have so much of this unusual taste was a chance not to miss.

It was one-thirty. The bar was closing. The wine was gone. Spector could not convince Humphrey to have a second kirsch. It wasn't that he didn't like them, you understand. Kit never finished the thought. His voice trailed off and his eyes roamed the ceiling. The he turned his face to Spector, senseless as a frog.

"I think it's time to go."

"Time to go," said Humphrey. When the big man tried to get up, he leaned on the circular cocktail table and it tipped. Spector caught both.

"Here we are," he said. "Lean on me."

The Humphreys had taken a small suite on the southeast corner of one of the hotel's higher floors. Spector had visited it before, not often, when they had invited him up for cocktails before dinner. Tonight he hoped that he could get his work done before arriving at the door, since encountering Devon would complicate matters. But it took two hands and all his wits, some of them straying down the somnolent path of his companion, to keep Humphrey propped against his shoulder and moving.

At the door he took Kit's key. Try as he might, he couldn't find an opportunity to free his hands. The slumping bodies brought Devon from her bed.

She peered through the peephole and opened the door. She wore a cream silk peignoir over a nightgown one shade lighter. She looked at Spector with a mix of emotions he could not read.

"Sorry to wake you. I thought Kit might need some help."

"I was up," she said flatly, and she reached for her husband's unsupported side.

Spector started to hand him over, but it was like steering a column of watermelons. Instead, wife and friend guided Humphrey into the bedroom. Without makeup and in the intimacy of the night, Devon looked even more vulnerable and no less appealing. Spector averted his eyes from her, concentrating instead on his objective. The appearance he gave in result convinced her anew that he was a gentleman.

The lights were out in the inner room of their little suite, and the bed, where Spector felt with his hand as he lowered Humphrey down, was warm from her body. He removed Kit's coat and carefully hung it in a closet. He removed the contents of the pockets, placing most of what he found in an orderly pile on the dresser.

He turned, walked to the bed, and removed the sleeping man's shoes. Then his tie. She stood at the door, her shadow on him.

He unlatched the belt and wondered how he could remove the trousers.

"Don't," she said. "Let him be."

He turned.

"That's all right. I'm not embarrassed."

"I am," she said.

156

She took his hand and led him away from the bedroom, shutting the door behind her. They walked to the front door of the suite. Spector held her hand. It was warm, the warmth of the body and the bed. He felt stirring in him an allure, a reprise of his feelings for her the night of the birthday party. Not whether but where. Here? With Kit in the next room? Back at his cottage outside Vevey? All the way back, to New York or Toronto or wherever was now home? It had been a long time, all the while waiting for a woman he would not see again, a woman who didn't know his name. It had been too long.

He kissed her, standing at the door. He kissed her deeply. In the next room Kit stirred and knocked something over. A lamp? A table?

She looked at him. "I've never cheated on him, you know. I don't have any idea why not."

And from inside they heard the siren of a telephone off its hook. That's what the bastard had knocked over. She spoke softly to him, holding the lapel of his jacket.

She went inside to aright the phone. Before she left she said, Wait here. He turned and closed the door quietly behind him.

He had set the alarm for six. But when it sounded, he wondered why, then, his thoughts recurring, wondered if he should scrap the whole idea. Easy to call up Devon, bring her back here, change his air reservations to Paris . . . He roused himself, washed, and peered at the guileless face in the mirror.

To make sure, he stuck two fingers into the breast pocket of the suit jacket he had worn last night. There, snug against his billfold, was the passport of Christopher Humphrey.

He dressed and packed a small briefcase. He would need no clothes. He drove his car through the November darkness toward Geneva, got an especially good parking spot, and reported to the gate. This was one of two early flights to London, and though the second would do, better to leave a margin of error.

He checked his watch at the gate. Too early, but necessary. He called the Palace and asked for the Humphreys' suite by number.

She answered.

"Devon . . ."

"Good morning."

"Look, about last night . . ."

"Thank you for bringing Kit home."

"Oh, sure. I'm sorry we caroused so."

"He's still asleep. It didn't seem to bother you. You sound as if you had a restful night."

"I had to get up early for that business appointment. Be in Geneva all day. Look, last night, as I was leaving, the bell captain downstairs caught me. Gave me Kit's passport. Just thought I'd mention it in case he's looking for it. I should have put it in your box, but I walked out with it."

"Oh. Thank you."

"I'll bring it back tonight or tomorrow."

There was a lengthy silence.

"Anything else?"

"What?"

"Did he lose anything else last night?"

"I don't think so," Spector said uncertainly. "Not that I found."

"Well, then." She sounded ingenuous. "I'm glad you were around."

25

Another wait at another airport. I could be happy as a monk if they'd promise me no line for vespers. He laughed to himself at the thought. From what

he had seen of the Church, an admittedly passing view, cele-
brants and penitents alike had to queue for every ministration.
No preferred treatment. Do you suppose heaven is like that?
And if so, how can it be heaven?

Customs and Immigration were crowded. With the first he
had the briefest interview. They looked quickly at the documents
in his case, noting the name of the prestigious law firm on the
stationery and the enclosure envelopes. They hadn't looked in
the accordion folder that fit in the top of the briefcase, but if
they had he was prepared with a verifiable explanation for carrying another man's passport. A sheaf of solicitor's documents
showed that he carried the man's power of attorney, a man with
whom he was this day embarking on a joint venture of consid-
erable substance.

He had decided to enter on his own papers—that is, for the
first time as Spector. He held two alternatives, both flawed. The
number on the Reade passport might be ranked on those lists
immigration people occasionally checked. Spector had settled so
comfortably in his role that he had to remind himself that the
Reade credentials were bogus. The Humphrey passport carried
a similar risk. It needed doctoring, a task that must be done
before presentation to Millington. The less work the better. A
simple paste-up would suffice for the lawyers. He would do that
after he had disembarked safely in England.

But he would enter as Spector. The face on the Humphrey
photo bore no likeness, he was pleased to note, to him; indeed,
the only described physical characteristic that Spector shared
with his dinner companion of the evening before was sex. More
accurately, gender. We could have shared something else, but I
opted for this appointment. It is a demanding life in which one
must decide between love and money.

So he presented his own document at the booth. For the
first time since he had hatched his scheme, his passport would
show an emigration, entering at Gatwick, leaving the next day.
Because he had long since decided that worry does not help, he
had given no thought to the possibility that someone might be
pursuing him, and though he would have acted no differently
had he been able to confirm his sense of security, he was in truth
out of harm's way.

Now, seated in the back seat of a taxicab, he set up shop.
He opened the top of his case to block the glance of the driver

159

in the rearview mirror, and then waited until the car rolled onto the smooth highway that, for a short stretch, was M23 to the north.

He removed the tube of water paste from his jacket and a spare passport photo from his wallet. Carefully he placed his picture over Kit's saturnine face. Close call, Humphrey. If you hadn't tossed in your sleep, I might have replaced you in the flesh. He dismissed the conjecture of why he had left Devon's room last night. As Cynthia said, try not to use the subjunctive.

They began to encounter the inevitable suburban traffic at Croydon. It was always a crowded and frustrating drive. Spector concentrated not on his nervousness but on the portfolio of documents he had brought. He realized that on several he had neglected to add Reade's signature, and, using a distinctive blue ink, wrote "Cyrus Reade" in a hurried but affirmative script. Then he removed the signature pages that Kit had signed and substituted the unmarked copies, so that he could execute those as Humphrey in the solicitor's presence.

The delays, forcing the cab driver into an erratic and anxious pace, gave Spector time to think of the next piece of the puzzle. He contemplated the agenda for the meeting. The transaction was the lawyer's show. Still, he wanted to be prepared.

The traffic had come to a halt. He looked at his watch, felt his stomach begin grinding in low gear. The second flight that morning went to Heathrow, farther out from London, but because of an easier commute it probably would have gotten him there about the same time. A frustrating speculation, made moot by the fact that he had time to spare. Nevertheless, there was a certain symmetry in being efficient.

They crawled through Brixton and Clapham. At last the car was into London, across the Southwark Bridge, and in view of Saint Paul's Cathedral. He had the driver drop him off at the east end of the church, close by his final destination. There he paused and considered the cathedral. He couldn't do otherwise. It was one of his favorite structures. In his earlier life he had worked on a merger with an English tin firm. When others broke for lunch, he came daily to the noon organ recitals. Now he stood outside the reconstructed American Memorial Chapel. There was the great dome, the dome whose dimensions and stolidity had come in his mind to represent the English character.

Someone—he'd forgotten who—had had to approve the original design, and the architect Wren had compromised with the shape. But he had gotten his marvelous dome.

One nice thing about my new career, he mused. No committees.

Despite the traffic, he was early. He walked unhurriedly down Cannon Street and paused when he saw, to the right, the Old Bailey. He determined not to go in. He had declined the airline breakfast, and he was hungry. Instead, with time to himself, he entered a pub on the corner. It was packed with a lunch crowd of clerks, court supernumeraries, and young barristers. The talk was of calendars, judicial assignments, and writs.

His hangover, mild in comparison to the one he assumed Humphrey had contracted, gave him a raging appetite. This place was populated; it must be good. He stepped to the tall glass counter. In it were several cold dishes. Behind, a steam table held a stew and several boiled vegetables. A large-bosomed woman with a graying mustache and her hair dyed yellow was serving customers at random.

"What'll it be?" she asked him before he had given the matter any thought.

"What's in the stew?"

"Little bit o' everything." She wiped her hands on her apron and rested the ladle she was using on her hip. It made a dark stain.

"I'll try that," he said, pointing to a plate of cold meats and loaves.

"That?" she asked, grabbing something else. "The pork pie." Before he could protest she had it on a plate and across the counter to him.

"Thanks," he said.

"Get your beer at the bar," she told him.

"Right."

He fetched a pint of Scotch ale, turned to the room, and searched out a table.

The pork pie was as close to inedible as anything he'd had since cooking for himself in New York. It was a single crust, sprinkled unhappily with pieces of lard. He could not decide whether, in the scheme of the pie, the meat was treasure trove or penalty.

He drank the ale, left most of the crust, and went back for a lemon pudding and coffee. The pudding was delicious, and his spirits brightened.

It was ten minutes of two. He told the cashier what he had bought, paid in American dollars, and left.

The day was gray and the slight wind cutting, but it was not unpleasant. Spector walked up to Newgate Street and back east toward the cathedral. One block and he was there.

The firm of Mason and Sample occupied a nondescript modern building on the south side of Newgate. Six or seven stories. Stationed in the lobby was a receptionist with a diary of the names of all persons expected upstairs. This was not a building where one dropped in to chat.

She looked like Deborah Kerr. To Spector every English-woman over forty looked like Deborah Kerr, those under like Audrey Hepburn. He inquired in his warmest voice whether Mr. Millington was in for Christopher Humphrey. She refused to lock eyes with him, sent him to five, and told him with a note of censure that Mr. Millington's secretary would be waiting.

He was led down the halls to a small conference room. A veneer table and cheap Danish furniture. What has become of the Jacobean carved oak of the Inner Temple? Or had that only been in Dickens?

Mr. Millington and his clerk, whom Millington briefly introduced, were waiting in the room. Mr. Millington was tall, perhaps six three, had a bony, stern face, which he regularly sprung into smile without reason. The result was consternation: one wasn't sure whether the owner of that face was aware of what was happening under, so to speak, his nose. Millington had brown-red hair, and that rubicund complexion that suffers in the sun. The clerk said nothing the entire meeting and continued to write furiously, no matter how trivial the conversation.

Lawyer and client chatted about Geneva and Saint Louis and London. About air travel and currency exchanges. Mr. Millington expressed again his regret at not being able to meet Mr. Reade. He had been informed by Crédit Suisse that Mr. Reade had made ready at least one million U.S. for this transaction. If Mr. Humphrey was satisfied, they could proceed.

Mr. Humphrey was satisfied. He produced from his brief-case his little agenda and the documents which, he told the so-

162

licitor, Mr. Reade had already signed before a notary. The solicitor was gratified by his clients' preparedness.

Millington began the explanation of the various pieces of paper. He had a deep and pleasant voice, and Spector was enjoying himself. The ale had made him mellow and just a little drowsy. At the proper time, as Mr. Millington requested, Spector handed Humphrey's passport to the clerk. The young man never looked at anything but the number, which he copied into his notes.

Millington presented the bank letter of instructions. Spector checked his notes.

"You need our account number, I assume."

"I do."

"Here it is." He handed Millington the bank card showing the account for Reade Holdings, 102 LE 2750.

"And so the entire two million U.S. will be transferred there."

"Precisely," Spector said, as an Englishman might. The clerk noted it down.

Millington was describing provisions of the company bylaws he might find of interest. Steam poured from the radiator in a hypnotic hiss. The secretary knocked and opened the door.

"Mr. Humphrey?"

"Yes?"

"Your wife is downstairs."

For the second that he sat silent, he wondered how he looked. He would never find out.

"Wonderful," he said. "Does she wish to come up?"

"I've asked her to," said the secretary. "May she join you?"

"Of course," said Millington. "What a pleasant surprise."

Spector grinned at everyone. Anything he might say had a good chance of proving wrong. They sat in silence.

Within minutes, there was a second knock on the door. Devon Humphrey entered. She wore a black skirt and a lavender tunic, and she carried a gray suede purse as if it were a favored book of poetry. Her beauty startled all three men, even Spector.

"Hello, dear," she said to him. "I hope you don't mind my popping in like this." She brushed her cheek chastely against his.

"Of course not," Spector said. "What a pleasant surprise."

The men jostled about to make room at the table, and Spector introduced her. Millington afforded her courtly and effusive treatment. He asked if she was interested in the transaction, and she assured him she was. And so, with Spector's approval, he went over the significance of each piece of paper. He had clearly enjoyed their authorship.

Devon played her part with equal thoroughness. She nodded at his words and occasionally cocked her head when legal or financial terms were used, causing Millington to explain his explanations. Her attentions encouraged the lawyer, and he went on. All the while, Spector regarded her with smiling eyes. Whatever trepidation he felt that her presence signified a purpose more devious than his was eclipsed by his admiration for her performance. And her performance was perfect. Not a glance, not a tone took him into her confidence. He wondered to himself, without any loss to his equanimity, who would ultimately be the victim.

"It really is all signed up now," Millington said at last.

"How exciting." She fingered through the papers. "You don't mind. . . ."

Millington showed by opened palms that he did not.

Now she opened her purse and removed a small tan folder. Spector recognized the bankbook of Crédit Suisse, doubtless the one sent directly to Kit. Devon had the deposit instructions in her other hand, and she was comparing numbers.

"Oh, look here," she said warmly. "You've made a mistake, dear."

"We have?" Spector asked with concern.

"You remember that Cy specifically said to put this money in LE 2749. Not the second account. The first account."

"He did?" asked Millington.

"Yes," she said. "I know he wouldn't want this money to go into the wrong account, would he, dear?"

"No," said Spector. "I had forgotten."

"Well, let me just correct that." Millington inked in the change. "We're glad you showed up, Mrs. Humphrey. That would have been an inconvenience for you."

"It certainly would have," Devon said.

Spector sat bemused, elbow on the table, his head resting on the crotch formed by his index finger and thumb. The smile on his lips could easily be read as spousal pride, rather than the discovery it in fact expressed. He noticed, as she turned her head, how her long neck muscles flexed down the collar of her tunic. That one million dollars was being moved with the correction of a number from his account to the fatuous Humphrey's did not compare in interest.

The clerk assembled sets of copies for Reade Holdings and for the Humphreys. Millington said, for security's sake, he would rather send his client's set directly, although he knew they were good friends. The Humphreys understood. They waited for the elevator.

"Are you staying in London long?"

"Oh, no," Spector answered. "We're going back . . ."

". . . tomorrow." She finished the sentence. "We're staying tonight at Claridge's. Kit has taken the bridal suite. A second honeymoon. Isn't that dear? He's quite a romantic, you know."

"Wonderful," Millington said, reddening. "I hope you enjoy yourselves. That is . . ."

"Oh, we shall, Mr. Millington. Put yourself at ease." And the conspicuous innuendo in Devon's voice accomplished, as she had intended, the opposite.

26

It was after seven that evening that they decided they needed air. Not exercise, air. The bedclothes and their own were scattered around the suite as if someone had done a search. Now they gathered up articles, trading with each other and giggling, until at last they were dressed sufficiently for a quick pass through the lobby.

The streets of Mayfair were quiet and the night air was cool. They held hands and walked so their shoulders touched. In flat shoes she was but slightly taller than he, and their bodies went together as if they had long been a team for the three-legged race at the fair.

"How did you find me out?"

"Gratitude."

He looked at her, not understanding.

"I didn't suspect you. I happened on you. I ran into Alfred at breakfast. He was passing through to the kitchen. I thanked him for returning Kit's passport to the bell captain, and he didn't know what I was talking about.

"Then I just added it up. Your wanting to go out with Kit alone, when it's obvious you can't stand him. Your being gone the next few days. The time set for the closing. I realized you had handled the whole London side of it."

"So I got the flight to Heathrow . . ."

"And tracked me down?"

". . . asked around to get the names of the largest law firms in London, and began calling. At first I was asking for Cy Reade, and then it occurred to me that I was looking for the wrong person. I started asking for Christopher Humphrey."

She smiled. She had a shy and hesitant smile. It suited her. Even at love, she was both passionate and demure. Spector found the combination alluring. She was eager to be taught, to be pleasing, to be pleased. Without asking, he sensed that her private life with Humphrey had frustrations equal to those of her public life, and that much of Kit's chatter substituted for action.

They walked west past Grosvenor Square and crossed the boulevard. Then they entered the park and went down the path he knew was called Lovers' Walk. She said, You're rhapsodizing, and he said, No, that's really its name, but she didn't believe him and preferred to think he had made it up. At the southeast corner of the park, they rounded the statue of Achilles.

They looked up at the figure of the greatest chieftain of the Greeks.

Devon said, "Make you want to go to war to kill Paris and bring back Helen?"

He thought a moment. "Makes me cold."

"Me too," she said. "Let's go back."

When they returned, a bottle of champagne in an ice bucket stood by their door, with a note from the manager. She had been chilled by their walk, and she ran a hot shower while he uncorked the wine and poured two glasses. She came out of the bathroom patting her long hair in a towel. She wore the peignoir she had worn the night before in Montreux—was it only then?— and around her neck a thin gold chain. He couldn't recall whether the chain had been there when they made love.

They sipped at their glasses. The wine was thin and sharp, and they put it down, preferring each other.

He lost track of sequence and frequency. There was a bath with overflowing bubbles, a series of gymnastic couplings. At two in the morning they both decided they were famished. The hall porter knew the name of an all-hours Chinese restaurant, and in a half-hour, a graceful, gray-haired waiter from the hotel delivered several white boxes on a serving cart. Mu shu pork, egg roll, fried rice, and raspberry sherbet. The staff had added a rose in a bud vase and, incongruously, the day's *Financial Times*. At some point they drank off the flattened champagne. It was surprisingly good mixed with the sherbet.

"Is Cy Reade your real name?" she asked him. It was the hour before dawn.

"It doesn't matter," he said.

"No." She held his hand and was examining his fingers. "But I would like to know something real about you. Besides this. Are you married?"

"No."

"Are you in love with someone?"

"Yes."

He felt her sigh.

"If only I were ten years younger, Cy Reade, and you were free."

"I am free," he said. His voice had a ring of melancholy, an oboe below the strings.

They both knew that she would be going back to Kit in the morning, and Spector simply didn't talk about him. It seemed indecorous to lure her into emotional infidelity. Then again, he was sufficiently pleased and sufficiently occupied with the physical brand.

They flew back to Geneva together. Once there, she decided to take the limousine to the hotel, rather than share his car. He nodded that he understood. He delivered her bags to the driver and helped her into the rear seat.

"Oh, Devon. I'll have to undo this Reade Holdings thing. It may work, but I'd hate to see Kit locked up for tax evasion. He won't mind, will he?"

Her expression showed her gratitude.

"He'll mind terribly. But I'll be relieved. Thank you. I never liked the scheme from the start."

"Well, then."

"Will we see you again?"

"Perhaps. We should have a farewell drink."

"You don't want to, do you?" She had guessed his thoughts.

"I feel as if I've been . . . undressed."

"Did you mind?"

"I didn't mind at all."

Humphrey was satisfied with the explanation. The money had arrived in Kit's Geneva account, and it was intact. But Reade's advisers had told him now was not the time to try this stunt, that the United States was becoming increasingly sensitive to large amounts disappearing, particularly in light of the recent indictments for insider trading.

"How 'bout those rascals?" Kit asked him. "Would you think some kid making those kinds of dollars would try to jew out a few more bucks on inside information? Greed has no limits, I guess."

Spector allowed as how he guessed too.

They had a last dinner together. Devon wore a blue wool dress, the color of her eyes, plain for a celebratory dinner, but Spector had made her promise he could see her in it. They had bought it in Knightsbridge, on the run, while the cab waited on the way to the airport. At the last minute they realized that she had to come back from an impromptu shopping trip with something in hand.

Kit was pleased. He expected his wife to indulge herself.

"That's what we get for our night out on the town, Cy. I

get the bills from Devon's trip. That's the way she takes revenge for my sowing some oats."

"Who got the better deal, then?" Spector said. He saw the smile in her eyes.

"No contest," Kit laughed. "I'll take that anytime. A night on the town against bills for a couple of dresses."

After dinner Spector declined a round in the bar. On balance, Humphrey was not disappointed; to the contrary, he seemed quite satisfied at his brush with international finance and tax evasion, and Spector guessed that he had gotten value for his money out of these months in Europe: a hypothetical and flawed scheme for cheating on taxes and a passbook at Crédit Suisse.

"Don't leave your money there," Spector warned him. "The Swiss are notoriously meager with interest rates." He shook Kit's hand and asked Devon if he might kiss her goodbye. Their lips touched lightly, and he was stirred by her scent and the memory of it.

He looked at her. "Tell me something."

"What?"

"Do you like Chinese food?" he asked.

"Love it."

He nodded his approval, and left them at the table.

"What was that all about?" Kit asked his wife.

"I don't really know. He's a bit of an eccentric."

"An odd bird," Kit agreed. "I'm not at all sure we know the real Cyrus Reade."

The next day the Humphreys checked out. They picked up their daughter in Lausanne and boarded a flight back to the States.

In Vevey, Spector's little house crowded down upon him. It was time to move on. He had rented it for six months, but the landlord would be happy to have it back. He seemed to be unable to fulfill lease commitments these days. First the Parishes' lovely home, now this.

"Is that you?"

"Yeah. How's it going?"

"Hey, I been waiting to hear. You get that crap I sent you?"

"Yeah. I got it. Look, Lauren. That second million? No go. I mean, I tried but no go."

"No sweat. We can still do the deal. But we're gonna have to move fast. They're getting ready to sell, and when they decide, I'd like to be there with the check."

"What's your timing?

"I think you ought to get your ass here. Right after Christmas or the New Year. I'd like to move before the whole reinsurance industry finds out about this and the price runs away from us." Spector's mind wandered to New York, his bare apartment.

"You there?"

"Yeah," Spector said, "I'm here. Just thinking. That's sooner than I had planned, but I'll tell you something. I'm homesick." He thought of the bullfight posters, of Billie Holiday singing. "Worst that happens is I defer a portion of the purchase price or pay higher taxes."

"Listen, Spector, income tax beats no income. Don't outsmart yourself. There's such a thing as too much brain power. Or, as we say in the ghetto, better to say 'I is rich' than 'I am poor.' "

Spector laughed. He had made up his mind. They rang off. Lauren's voice brightened his spirits. To be distinct one had to be apart. Sometimes it got lonely.

He punched in another number.

"I'm sorry, sir. We have no listing at that address."

"Try Manhattan."

"I'm sorry, sir. We have . . ."

"Do you have any Olives listed? Brooklyn or New York."

"Yes, we do, sir."

"Look, operator. This is an overseas call. I can't afford to play 'Jeopardy.' You have the answers, I have the questions. Do you have any Olives like the ones I'm looking for?"

"I have an Olive, C., in Brooklyn. Park Slope."

"That's it. That's the one."

"I'm sorry, sir. The customer has requested that we not give out that number."

27

The day before he was to leave Vevey he spent walking amid the parks and public gardens of the town. The day was overcast, and an occasional fleck of snow spotted the dark-gray cheviot weave of his overcoat. After three, almost four, months, he had become sufficiently acclimated to Switzerland that not every pedestrian looked like the secretary of a legation, a fugitive financier, or a Baltic émigré. The streets of Vevey were filled with people who did nothing more than live in Vevey.

Logic suggested that he should now find it easy to pass merely as one of the people who live in New York. This had been a suitable land to catch one's breath in before going on. Had it been Marx or Engels who had lived here? He was not suited to exile. He needed roots, companionship, and the steady nourishment of his own culture.

He gave himself a final indulgence. He had hoped to find a pleasant resort where he would be warm. But the Mediterranean was unreliable in December, and the better Caribbean resorts had long been filled. He determined to spend Christmas skiing.

He took a room at a little ski town not three hours' drive from Vevey. His lodgings were cramped, but he spent his days on the mountain and his nights at the bars and restaurants. He was able to rent an entire outfit, of far better quality than what he owned at home. He met people without effort: the chair lifts accommodate two or more, and conversation is easy for the ride up the mountain. In the evenings one came upon friends made on the trails that day and, if not, one could rely on the passing camaraderie of the day's sport. Spector made several casual acquaintances and rarely dined alone.

At first the rush of the activity satisfied him. His skiing was adequate, no better. He could descend most slopes, but he rapidly lost grace and confidence as the land fell away and the moguls sprang out at him. He was athletic and it stood him well, and yet the long absence from any activity more vigorous than portaging Kit Humphrey or cycling around the mountain paths had weakened him. Basically fit, after two or three days he was able to ski from morning to the close of the lifts. He enjoyed the air, the speed, the increasing sense of gyroscopic balance that must be something like flight.

But the conversations, at first welcome, fast became tedious. Snow conditions, the cities of origin, the comparative difficulties of the pitches. As his legs strengthened, he imagined his brain turning to the farina that so many of the Germans had for their breakfast, a white, pasty colloid that could not support itself outside the bowl.

He bought current French novels at the stores in town and resolved to begin reading in earnest. He bought a tablet of writing paper and resolved to chart out the alternatives for his life. There would be a decision tree, a series of matrices, starting with the company Lauren was pursuing—one branch if they made the deal and one if they didn't. If they made the deal, whether he would work with the company or not. If not, what he would do with himself. Eventually the branches of the tree disappeared into uncharted regions.

He allocated time for his project, the way a camp counselor might assign housekeeping chores. But after a day outdoors, a whiskey at the bar, a glass of wine, and a homey, ample dinner, Spector went back to his room and crawled into bed. The novels of passion and intensity seemed irrelevant to his life, equally irrelevant as the way he'd been living.

He needed another destination.

Spector celebrated the New Year with two dozen people he didn't know. The Americans were busy kissing each other's wives, the few Swiss were busy dancing, and the Germans were disapproving of both. He skied on New Year's Day, bright blue with new powder that sprayed in his wake. The next day, a Tuesday, he decreed to be devoted to work. On a rented typewriter he drafted some legal documents. Then, as Humphrey, he called Millington in London. Reade and he had decided to dismantle Reade Holdings. Millington should assume it would be dormant and eventually disqualified unless Millington heard differently.

The solicitor was not pleased. He said it was all a bit irregular, particularly in light of their having paid his statement for services so promptly. Yet, after all, they were the clients.

The next morning Spector took his documents into town, found a *notaire,* and with the signing of a few pieces of paper concluded the sale of all of the outstanding shares of Spector Peripherals, all owned by himself, to one Cyrus MacNeil Reade for $1.46 million. That was the balance of the money Reade had left in his Geneva bank. It closed the account.

No, Mr. Reade assured the concerned official. He had no worry that Spector's signature was not on these documents. His counsel across the Atlantic had taken care of that part of the closing several days ago. Reade was confident he would shortly have documents bearing Spector's hand as well as his own.

The *notaire* was quite agreeable to the request of Mr. Reade, for that was the passport Spector showed him, to instruct the bank to forward the proceeds to a Panamanian trust set up for just this purpose. No need to involve Mexico this time. Panama was instructed that the money would be drawn out by its owner when he returned to the United States and completed banking arrangements. No need for the melodrama of code names. Panama should expect the instructions to come from New York, from a man named Spector.

Finally Spector stopped in at a travel agency and made arrangements to fly from Zurich to JFK. The next direct flight was full. He boarded the following day.

New York

28

It was a dilemma. Both passports were flawed. He fingered them nervously in his suit pocket, trying to decide. In any event, the way to get through was to act perfectly cool. Immigration and Naturalization Service: one line for U.S. citizens, a shorter line for everyone else. He studied the faces of the two agents. The woman handling the long line looked like a grammar-school teacher who had taught him long division. The young man with the Jerry Colonna mustache had a dreamy look, placid.

No, Spector was telling him, he didn't have a green card. He was merely coming through New York on his way to Toronto. A passing business transaction.

The man pulled one of several clipboards from his drawer. On it was a long list. Somehow Spector knew he was on it.

If he used his own passport he risked discovery that its owner had never left the country. No exit stamp. Tiny beads of sweat formed on his upper lip. He was reading upside down, faster than the agent. Then again, he knew what he was looking for. The list was first by name, then by number. His eyes scanned ahead. There it was. FEADE, CYRUS MACNEIL.

"Oh, Christ."

The young officer looked up.

"Sir?"

"I forgot to declare this watch," Spector said. He showed the man his wristwatch, seven years old. He hoped it was Swiss.

"That's not INS. That's Customs."

"Can't you do that for me? I really don't want to break the law."

"Sorry, sir. You'll just have to wait and go back to Customs." The officer thought the Canadian was genuinely concerned.

"It was a gift. From my lover."

The man looked at him. He wasn't looking for a debate. "Sorry, sir. Customs will handle it."

"I'll have to go back and explain. I'd hate for them to seize it or anything. Frederick would never understand."

The man regarded him more closely.

"Please let me go tell them. I don't want to get into any trouble over this."

The officer sucked in his lower lip, showing the edge of his front teeth.

"Of course. You go back to that office by the baggage racks. See it? You tell them about Frederick."

"Thank you. Thank you very much."

Spector went back to the office. He made out an amending customs declaration. He noted the watch as a gift, and estimated its value at five hundred dollars.

"That watch is old," said the puzzled customs officer.

"Well, Frederick couldn't afford a new one," Spector explained.

They checked the tariffs on used jewelry and computed the amount. Spector paid in U.S. currency. He had changed all of his traveler's checks at the airport and had withdrawn the little left in Reade's demand account in dollars.

He reapproached the INS desk.

"Thank you so much. They couldn't have been nicer."

"Glad to be of help, Mr. Reade," the young man said. Spector walked through his gate and out to the terminal to claim his baggage.

How can you be elated to be back in a three-room, whitewashed apartment that costs you eleven hundred dollars a month? Where you have to turn on the lights and wait a split second before entering to let the roaches scurry out of sight?

Spector was. In the living room sat the upholstered Queen Anne in its gleaming brocade, and one of the chrome chairs from the dinette set. Each sat by a coffee table. The furniture looked like the first props of an amateur theatrical.

Someone had organized the mail on the kitchen table. It could only have been Lauren or the woman who came in to straighten up. Probably her. Ah, yes. He had let her go. Nothing left to straighten. Must have been Lauren.

He had arranged four months' mail, not by date, but by importance. All the third-class, unsolicited, was in one pile. The magazines in a second. There were damned few first-class, white envelopes. Most of those were computer-addressed. It said, he thought, something about his life. The vast majority of my correspondents are third-class.

In his absence, several of his memberships had lapsed. The Museum of Modern Art, the Smithsonian. Nowhere that would not be happy to take him back.

Not so the Racquet Club. A lapse there would get him posted in two months, ousted in three. He had left envelopes for Lauren with his monthly dues and a little extra. The club's antiquated accounting system was forever picking up charges two or three months after they'd been incurred, and he didn't want to get bounced over an unpaid bar bill.

The truly personal mail was sparse. A few invitations never declined, long since expired. A note from Sonya, the advertising girl, saying she hoped he would call again when he wasn't so distracted, and a letter whose strong, perpendicular printing he recognized immediately. No greeting, it plunged into its message:

Where are the files for that gold-trading account we had? You remember that's mine under the settlement, plus the losses. My accountant needs the statements.

Joan

A warm and compassionate woman, Joan. He laughed and stuck her note on the pile of unsolicited junk.

He was exhausted from his trip. One last call before a mid-afternoon nap.

"You back?"

"I'm back. You're off garbage duty."

"You ready to roll on this deal? How does it look?" Lauren was eager. This was his stimulant.

"Looks good to me. Somehow we'll have to raise a second

179

million or convince them to take less down. If I had to guess, I'd say it will be a little of both."

"Fine. What happens next?"

"Next we sit down and plan out our approach. How's Saturday?"

"Suits me fine. Too bad we can't hit a tennis ball first."

Spector looked outside and saw sleet passing in front of a yellow brick wall that was the neighboring apartment house. Then he looked down. In his hand was a mailing from his club.

"Hey. Meet me at the northwest corner of Fifty-third and Park, Saturday, ten-thirty. Bring your gear. I'll book a court for a couple of hours and we can talk after that."

"Can't fool me, man," Lauren said. "Ain't no schoolyard there."

"We'll think of something."

"You any better than you were last time?"

"I'm a lot better," Spector said. "Richer, smarter, better. But my tennis is about the same."

29

On Friday, before his match, he put himself through a light workout. Calisthenics, a two-mile jog around Riverside Park, stretching. He felt limber, but he reminded himself not to expect too much. His game would surely suffer for having been dormant these months. And remember to hit through on the backhand. The last time he forced you, drove through and deep, and didn't give you a chance to set up. When that happens, you hit out from the forearm, you get no shoulder or body behind it. The result is a chop, an undercut. The ball hits the ground spinning at the hitter, not away, the bounce is soft and predictable, and your opponent moves in like a hawk on a rabbit.

Rabbits don't win. The best a rabbit can do against a hawk is a tie.

If you'll just keep to the jogging regimen, you'll get up to five miles in no time. Add a quarter-mile a day. Two weeks.

After a shower, he called his neighborhood bank to arrange for an account. The last in this series. Now he could pull the money back from Panama in his own name, pay the taxes on it, and use the rest as he saw fit. After everything, he'd have over a million. A million one seventy. Lauren's deal would take up most of that. Still, not a bad position to be in at thirty-one, pressing thirty-two. Seven figures in the bank, free and clear. If only his backhand would hit out.

The young man on the telephone was pleasant, accommodating. A Mr. Kamenfeld. Yes, they could handle that size of account and make certain it got into insured deposits. He discussed yields and the length of deposit and the handling of the paperwork. They would be happy to help him on Saturday. Kamenfeld would be there to supervise it personally, and he had a new clerk who was very good and would set everything up. And he himself would oversee the transfer from Panama on Monday.

That would be fine, Spector told him.

Nice to be treated like a hot shot. Nothing like money to get people's attention. Them that's got shall get.

Early the next day, Saturday, he walked down Broadway, stopping at several wire trash baskets to discard the last pieces of Cyrus Reade. The second half of several credit cards, receipts from Geneva, the remaining pages of a Canadian passport. It was a blustery day. The wind blew away the sun's warmth and sharpened its light. Spector squinted against the rays, against the chill, against the flying debris. New York was dirtier than he remembered, and the West Side particularly so, hostile, impersonal, without grace. And he wouldn't trade it for all the wines of Switzerland.

He made an odd figure among the swirls of paper. He wore a camel's-hair topcoat that he had not taken abroad, a white wool turtleneck sweater, gray slacks, and moccasins. He carried a canvas tennis bag, a leftover from his college days. It still bore the college sticker and seal. Did he cling too much to the past? Only the good parts. He was free, he thought, free not only of his relationship with Joan but of the ennui that had caused it to fail. His parents had molded him to Fabian views. And although he had countered that trend by living first as a plutocrat and than off the plutocrats, that counterreformation had now ended. He had the happy independence of no political slant. Neutrality. It's like a new start. Who could ask for more?

Funny, he thought. Now that I'm changed, would Joan and I make a go of it? At the point where a man doesn't care whether his wife wants out or not, wouldn't any sane woman want out?

The bank was at the corner of Seventy-second and Broadway. It was the main branch of a small New York chain. Right next door was the deli where he and Shelley had had lunch so often.

Saturday commerce was going on with a reduced staff. Mostly people waited sullenly in line for a teller so they could withdraw moneys for the weekend. Spector asked the guard for Mr. Kamenfeld. A young man, his height and age and maybe twice the weight, came out from the back, hand extended. He wore a gray vee-neck sweater under his brown suit and smelled of nasal spray. Not exactly banking at Morgan. Still, he had everything ready, and handled the prospective depositor like an important addition.

He showed Spector how the money would be placed for immediate yield. Then he dispatched him to the new-accounts desk, where Spector was to fill out some forms. Spector walked to the rear of the large, open room that was the bank's main floor. There a woman sat, her back to him, pecking away at a typewriter.

He went over and stood, waiting for her to turn around.

"Excuse me. My name is Spector. Mr. Kamenfeld said you could finish the work on this new account."

The woman stopped typing but remained facing the wall. Spector had a sudden dread that something was wrong, that he had walked into a trap. For weeks he had not troubled himself with the chance of capture, having decided at the outset that thought and caution would produce safety, that worry produced only more worry. But, standing there, facing this frozen back, he felt a shiver of fear and had a sudden urge to run.

Slowly the woman turned in her swivel chair.

It was Cynthia.

"Hello, Mr. Spector. Mr. Kamenfeld said you'd be coming in."

He had no words. None. If she were as flustered, she was the greater actor. She pulled a bunch of forms from her desk drawer, slid off the paper clip, and started explaining them to him. He didn't hear a thing she said.

After she had spoken, she looked up at him, and he realized he was supposed to respond, to give her information, probably to sign something.

"What do I do now?" he asked.

"You fill in these papers, as I was saying, and sign where the yellow tabs are."

She handed him a straight pen, one from the stand on her desk, and he signed in response to her moving red fingernail. He never looked at a word.

"Mr. Spector, you'll have to fill in the blanks too."

"I've got to speak to you," he said.

"We'll need you to give us authorized signatories, Social Security, designation of beneficiary."

"Can you get out of here?"

"We close at one on Saturdays."

"Dinner."

"Sorry," she said. "Last time I dated a bank's customer it cost me several nights' sleep and a job."

"Cynthia, for Christ's sake, have dinner with me."

She looked at him, studying his earnest face. Spector could not read whether her motive was curiosity or affection, and he did not care. She reached into her desk and took out a large envelope for his copies of the documents. Carefully she closed its flap and wound the red string around the cardboard disk.

"You know the seal pool?"

"What?" He didn't understand.

"The seal pool. By Fifth Avenue. The zoo's reopened."

"The zoo. In the park."

She nodded. "Meet me at two. I can't stay long. I have a

date." She handed him the envelope and swiveled in her chair so that her back was to him once more.

He left and went out headlong into a gust of soot.

"You're really a schizophrenic. Several different personalities. Was it Jekyll or Hyde?"

"It was both. They were the same man. Dr. Jekyll and Mr. Hyde."

"Well, Jekyll couldn't play for the Lighthouse, and Hyde beat the shit out of me today."

They were sitting in the locker room. They had played only two sets, because their court time was limited. Lauren had trounced him six–one in the first. In the second Spector had trailed four love, and had come back to win in fourteen games. He had been superb.

They sipped their drinks. He had made a shandy for Lauren, mixing a beer with ginger beer, and drank a grape juice from the bottle. The cooler in the locker room was on the honor system; one merely helped himself and wrote out a ticket. The room itself was extraordinary. It had a high ceiling, twenty or twenty-five feet, from which there depended metal-shaded lamps, the kind you imagine over pool tables. The walls were all paneled, and the lockers themselves were paneled doors set flush into the stained wood. The result was a darkened room filled with towels, the smell of liniment, the glisten of racquets. Spector didn't care one way or the other about his membership, but he loved this room. The lighting, the forms, the colors, it was his private Bellows painting.

They had played their match to an audience of a half-dozen members, two waiting to get on, two coming off a squash court, the others idling away a January Saturday until the bar opened. To Spector's surprise and, he realized later, disappointment, his inclusion of a black man as a guest was challenged by no one. Indeed, there was no mention of it, and their reception was of the identical dissociability—neither friendly nor hostile—that he had come to know over the years.

In the shower he deliberated on this morning. He had been obsessed with finding Cynthia again. Surely this meant there would be something permanent between them. She was not nearly so indifferent about him as that interview had indicated. Those three days, even for a woman as worldly as she, had been special. Once he had reached that conclusion, midway in the second set, he found the concentration necessary to return Lauren's service. The rest of it he had done on adrenaline, pumping through his body like a downpour through an arroyo. He had played on a high.

The shower stalls in the locker room were marble slabs, and in each shower was a stone bench. From a height of almost nine feet, the water sprayed out of oversize steel heads. They were fixtures in construction not seen for forty years. In the past, pricked by his bank account or social conscience, Spector had considered at times giving up his membership. Each time the thought of these luxurious showers persuaded him to stay.

He lay on the bench and let the water pound his back. After ten minutes he dragged himself up, shut down the water, and came out. Lauren was sitting on his bench, the water hitting his neck, his long arms draped to the ground.

"Man, you can't get me out of here. This is better than sex."

Funny, Spector thought. Until I saw her again today, I would have said the same thing.

30

The cold was sharp, and he stood by the entrance to the zoo blowing on his fists. Once she came, he thought no more about the weather. She was precisely on time. She wore a green loden coat with a high military collar turned up against the wind. From the redness in her nose and high cheeks he guessed she had walked from the crosstown bus.

"Come," he said with a parietal air. "Let's have lunch."

"No. I've eaten. I want to watch the seals."

Few people were out of doors. The wind gusted, and the bright sky made it hard not to squint.

The sea lions lay on the top of the sculpted rocks in the center of the pool. The largest, a male, was in ill temper, and moved his fat and black shining bulk only to push away the other two.

"No show today."

"They get fed at one," she said. "After that they just hang around waiting for the next feeding."

He took Cynthia's arm and they walked past other animals. A polar bear eyed them with diffidence. The Gentoo penguins, for whom the weather seemed suited, stood phlegmatically by.

"Slow day," Spector said. "How about coffee?"

She agreed. They entered the cafeteria, where he hoped to find a quiet place to talk. The room was filled with parents and their children, salvaging a cold outing with hot chocolate, puddings, ice-cream bars.

She found the only empty table, and he brought over two mugs. Finally he would have her to himself.

As he sat down, a gray-bearded man in a stocking cap and pea jacket came to their table. He carried his own mug, dangling the flap of a tea bag.

"Is this seat taken?"

Spector said yes and Cynthia said no, simultaneously. The man smiled graciously at her, sat down, and removed his hat and two fingerless gloves.

"Don't worry," he said to Spector. "I just came in to get out of the cold. Won't be long." He wrapped his hands around the white mug. After a moment, he reached for the sugar, methodically tore three packets at the corner, and, holding them as one, poured them into his mug. Then he reached into his coat and removed a wooden contraption. It had four handles across a spool strung with twine. It might have been for holding a kite.

Spector and Cynthia watched him. He tinkered with the machine, and with the glistening lead weight at the end of its line.

186

Spector knew he had lost. "What," he asked, "is that?"

"That's for fishing," the man said amiably.

"Fishing for what?" Cynthia drew in to the table.

"Coins, lady. Sometimes tokens, credit cards. I even got a ring once on Seventh and Thirty-third."

"Down grates," Spector deduced. "You hang the line down grates."

"You got it, mister. The deeper the better. Keeps away the competition. Most of my competition don't have my steady hand."

"And," Cynthia said, fingering the plumb weight on the end of the line, "that's a magnet. You lower it down and it holds on and you pull it in."

"Sorry, lady. Not so good. Coins aren't metal any more. I use stickum. Vaseline usually. In cold weather like this you got to cut it with soap. That'll pick it up."

They introduced themselves. He gave his name as Winston, although he didn't say whether that was a first or a last name. Winston was happy to talk about his profession. The choice spots were where people handled money. That's what made the job challenging, if you could figure out new fishing holes. Bus stops, subway stations, parking meters were obvious ones. But when the Met had had the Renoir show, people lined up around the block. The Van Gogh show wasn't so good. Admission was a flat five dollars. No silver.

And the seasons. Summer you had tourists, and they were great at losing things. Winston had a low regard for out-of-towners. Then it was slow again until winter.

"Why winter?"

"Gloves, lady. People wear gloves, they drop things. All the time. Keys, cigarette lighters. But people nowadays don't use fancy lighters. Just Bics. It's a pity. Used to be, in the best days, people carried cigarette cases."

Zoos were good too, he assured them. "But you want a real zoo, you gotta go to the Bronx."

"More volume," Spector added helpfully. But Winston was off on another tack.

"Ever wonder why they call it 'the Bronx'? Nobody calls it 'the Queens' or 'the Staten Island.' "

Winston finished his tea, took several packets of sugar for

his pockets, and put on his coat. They wished him luck. He walked out into the closing light.

"He's right," Cynthia said. "I've never thought of that. Why do you suppose that is?"

"Cynthia, give me a minute, will you? Forget about the Bronx. Don't you want to hear what this was all about?"

"Oh, I know what it was all about. It was about jabbing Empire State for about one and a half mil."

Spector made her promise not to move or give away another seat. He got two refills, came back, and sat down.

He hadn't had time to create a story or to think through what to say. She knew he wasn't Edgar Parish. He started there.

She listened in good humor, but offhandedly, as if she were at a family reunion with a distant cousin she used to play with as a child. Spector tried to close the gap with candor. It was an unfamiliar tactic, and he couldn't decide whether it was having any effect.

As he spoke, she seemed to warm to the words. Was it to him? To his wit? His predicament? Spector couldn't tell. He kept talking. Before long he had told her the whole story. The ads, the breakfast with the Parishes, the wire transfers, the cuts taken in Mexico and in Panama, the names of the contacts, and the size of their fees. He even told her something about the broken deal in Geneva, and about Kit Humphrey bumbling around, waiting to be taken the next time.

"I can't tell you how often I thought of calling. I didn't care whether it would trip me up. There I was, sitting in that lovely city in that lovely country with a packet in the bank. It was like living in a film strip you saw in grammar school. And you were here. You were in the audience."

She watched him, and he wanted to read how he was doing in her face, but she gave no sign, no reassurance. She had the street's suspicion of strong, unselfish emotions, and he would do well to stay away from them until later. If there were to be a later.

"I should have known you were a phony," she said amiably. "Why?"

If nothing else, he thought he had been clever. For her to be second-guessing that now offended his sense of accomplishment.

"I didn't know at the time. But nobody who isn't somebody

188

calls up the River Cafe on a Friday night and gets a window table. Specially nobody from Illinois."

They laughed. Two kids at the next table were fighting over animal crackers. One had eaten the other's hippo. Perhaps it was not irretrievable after all.

She told him about losing her job, having this dreadful fellow from the insurance company follow her, hit on her. First he wanted to arrest her. Then to bed her. She didn't like either pitch. Then there was the story in the papers. Bank employees questioned in swindle. A little article, but it's amazing who reads the *Times*. It was enough. She delisted her phone, found a new apartment nearby, and spent two months pounding the pavement. The job she had was a significant demotion. Less money, less title. But it was a job, and she'd work her way out of it soon enough.

He started to sniffle, a slight cold brought on by leaving his shower into the harsh winter's day. Cynthia fussed over him and teased him and he started to feel good about the future. He told her about the money coming in from Panama, about Lauren and the deal he had found. She listened. Mostly she listened. Had she always been so reactive, and he hadn't noticed?

"Say something, will you? I'm busting my ass to impress you with my honesty. I mean, look at me. I'm riding no hands."

She nodded in thought.

"I'm impressed," she said. But he couldn't tell what she was thinking.

She insisted she had to go. They walked up the stairs past the arsenal and out to Fifth. In the dimly lit sky of late afternoon hung the moon, slim as a potato chip. No, she would not let him take her home to Brooklyn. In compromise, she let him send her in a cab. He gave the driver a twenty and told him self-consciously to take the lady where she wanted to go.

She sat in the rear seat, her feet on the threshold. Spector held the door open, leaning on it. It was too early to know, she said. Maybe this will work, maybe not. She wasn't even sure they had stopped watching her. They ought to look out, just in case. Keep their distance for a while.

He agreed. He agreed that he sounded like a cold. He agreed to go home and take two aspirin.

"Look, Cynthia. I'll leave my body to Mayo's. I'll agree to anything. I'm desperate. Have dinner with me next week."

"Mortimer's," she said. "Seven-thirty, next Saturday."

He seated her in the cab and bent to kiss her. It was a gentle and tentative kiss. The softness of her lips reminded him why he had come back.

31

He picked up the telephone on Monday morning at eight-thirty sharp.

"Hi. You work fast. Let me get my coat off. I haven't done anything about Panama."

"I'm not calling about Panama. I'm calling about us. And I can't call you at home, 'cause you haven't given me your new number."

"All in time. Look, while I have you. That other stuff we need for your account."

She asked questions and he gave her the data. He felt foolish, as if he were asking that she mend his socks. Moving the money, the entire deal with Lauren seemed so commercial, suddenly extraneous. Cynthia noted all the details and told him the account would be ready to go that morning. He could go ahead and give wire instructions. After their business was done, she begged off, pressed by an appointment with her boss. She would see him Saturday night.

Spector threw himself into the reinsurance acquisition. He was back in his old form. He and Lauren clearly had a jump on the opposition. The owners hadn't shopped the company, and maintained that if they could get a fair price they saw no need to do so. They had several requirements of Spector, among them evidence of his capability to go forward. He gave them Kamenfeld's name, with whom, he told them, he had just completed arrangements for a certificate of deposit in excess of a million dollars. That same day they checked the reference, and Kamenfeld backed him up. Dealing in truths was easy.

There were the usual points to be worked on. Lauren and Spector examined the stability of the business, the threat of undisclosed liabilities, whether the relationships with the primary carriers would survive a change in ownership. They inquired into the soundness of each insurance syndicate and whether any existing reinsurance contracts would come back to haunt them. They were a good pair. Lauren understood the substance of the business they were buying and he understood something about how to buy a company.

"Remember," he told Lauren, "we think we know why we're buying. But the seller knows for sure why he's selling."

It was a satisfying week. Every morning Spector ran in the park, increasing his distance by a quarter-mile. Maybe being a legitimate capitalist wasn't as dull as I first thought. Maybe a lot depends on whom you're doing it with. And for. Have I hit upon a new economic theory? Wait till I tell J. S. Mill. I've outdone all those social philosophers knocking themselves out to come up with a world view. Of course, they've never made love to Cynthia.

His days were spent at the target company, asking questions, gathering data. He had turned on the lawyers—he used the same fellow who had recommended Millington in London—and there were draft acquisition agreements and tax plans to be studied. In the evening Lauren and he met at Lauren's midtown office, where they analyzed the facts they had been given and ran projections of what could happen to their new company in the best and worst of cases.

During these sessions Lauren was rarely anything but serious. None of the street slang and mock-hip attitudes of the tennis courts. His work was thoughtful, incisive. Spector was reminded of himself, breaking into the big time. Give me a chance and I'll run on top of the water.

Spector's mother and father had preached to him the futility of a life that was not of service to others. And although he had long since discarded that as a personal ideal, he believed it a sound business precept. He began analysis of any company, whether for his own acquisition or for a client, with that investigation. How desired was this company? Did it fill a real need? How strong was the demand for the job it did, and what part of that demand was stimulated by its own propaganda? You can convince people to try a toothpaste in three colors by giving it away. At some price you might convince a few of them to buy it. But, left to their own devices, they would not call you up in the dead of night and ask for it.

One by one the tasks on Spector's list were lined off. When Lauren and he broke the news to the sellers that they proposed only a million down, to their relief there was no panic, no rejections. An adjustment in the purchase price was negotiated. The buyers agreed to pay the second million out of their first earnings, and to grant the sellers a lien on the company's assets in preference to all other creditors. Lauren and he then huddled with their credit provider and talked the lenders into taking a second position. It wasn't easy.

Not easy, except compared with getting a table at Mortimer's for Saturday night. The restaurant was famous not for its food but for its inhospitability. It was a celebrity spa, and it maintained its reputation by allowing only a handful of the gawkers to mix with the objects of display. Spector went through every contact he could think of, finally calling upon the senior partner of the firm he had worked for. The old gentleman obliged, cautioning that he shouldn't expect a preferred seating.

Despite his rushed schedule and his anxiety to move it along, Saturday turned up in its usual order. He arrived at the restaurant fifteen minutes ahead of the time for his rendezvous. He wanted no recent VIP to take his slot. The maître d' listened to his name.

"Oh, yes, Mr. Spector. We've taken the liberty of seating someone else at your table."

"What?"

"We assumed you would not be needing it. You got your note, I hope?"

"What note?"

"Perhaps," the waiter said, with ostensible pity, "perhaps the coat-check girl didn't know you. She has a message for you."

He went back to the front. He was in a rage. Why had they read the note? It was in a sealed white envelope, with the restaurant's embossed logo on the flap. Not in Cynthia's handwriting. Clearly she had called it in.

He opened it and the girl, unasked, got his coat from its hanger.

Dearest—
    I've come down with your cold after all. No precaution too great. Excuse me this time.
    Gezundheit and

love—
C.

How like her. How enraging and ambiguous. Would there be a next time? She doesn't say. And on second reading calming and clear. Or, rather, parts of it. The salutation and the signing off . . .

No matter. He took his coat and left. He had no way to locate her until Monday. Gezundheit. God bless.

32

He hopped a Broadway bus headed south. He could walk but, given his excitement, he'd doubtless run, and it was too early in the day to break into a sweat. The weather had warmed, and he was overdressed in scarf, topcoat, gloves. The bus was hot enough to bake bread. By Seventy-ninth Street he could feel the wetness in the small of his back

Still, he had great news. Lauren had talked to the sellers yesterday—Sunday—and had been told it looked as though the deal would go. They would work toward a contract-signing the end of this week and a closing in a month. He and Lauren would be in business together. A new chapter, a new life.

He walked briskly into the bank, shedding his coat. Cynthia would be excited too.

Somebody else was at her station in the back. His heart sank. Was something wrong? He went up to her, a chubby girl with a large beauty mark on her cheek.

"Miss Olive," he said. "Is she around?"

"No. She's on vacation this week."

Spector's apprehensions disappeared, and he was left with the disappointment that he couldn't share his news.

"You sure? You must be mistaken. She didn't say anything."

"I didn't talk to her. She called our supervisor, Mr. Kamenfeld?"

"Oh, yes. Is he around?"

The girl shrugged and picked up her phone. Spector fiddled with a letter opener, drumming it on the fake-walnut veneer. The girl glanced at him and he stopped.

Kamenfeld came out. Spector shook the beefy hand he extended.

"Mr. Spector. Good to see you again. No need, of course. Cynthia gave me explicit instructions about your account."

"This young lady said she's on vacation."

"No, no," Kamenfeld said. Spector was reassured. She would have said something if she'd been planning a break. At dinner or in her note.

"Not to worry. She's taken care of everything. She called on Friday to tell me she had taken care of everything. She was out Friday, sick."

"I knew she was sick," he said. "And she's still on sick leave?" Will he let me have her home address?

"No. Not sick. Gone. Gave her notice."

He felt the sweat form again, first in the small of the back, then on the upper lip.

"Notice."

194

"Gave her two weeks. Last Monday, a week ago today. She had one week of vacation coming, so she took it for her second week. You can do that. Bank policy."

Spector stood looking at him. He brought the man's face in and out of focus, seemingly at will. Kamenfeld must have thought he wanted to know more, so he volunteered.

"She was a real find. I'm going to miss her."

"Mr. Kamenfeld," he said shortly, "do you suppose we could take a look at my account?"

"Of course. Come this way."

He led Spector to a waist-high gate. A buzzer sounded from afar, unlatching the door. Kamenfeld held it open for him. At the very rear of the bank were three or four windowless offices. They went into one. There were pictures of little children, all looking like Kamenfeld.

"We'll have to pull it up on the screen," he said. "We're all computerized now, but it means we can't get paper statements until the end of the month."

Kamenfeld tapped at the keys of the terminal on his desk. He spelled Spector's name out loud as he entered it.

"Yes. That's right."

"Here it is, then."

They leaned close to the screen to look. The printing was white against the illuminated green background. It appeared to shimmer for a moment, then lock in place. As if floating up from the depths.

DATE	ENTRY	DEBIT (CREDIT)
1-13	TFR—Primero Banco Comml (Pnm)	$1,174,420.07
1-13	Wire transfer fee	(25.00)
1-17	TFR—Primero Banco Comml (Pnm)	(1,174,420.07)
1-17	Wire transfer fee	(25.00)
1-20	Interest to date (5 days @ 5.1%)	820.89
1-20	Balance to date	$770.89

Spector stared. The numbers didn't change.

"Would you like me to print this out?" Kamenfeld asked.

"No," he said. "I think I have it." He took a breath and stepped back. "Mr. Kamenfeld. Do you think I might see the underlying stuff on this account? The signature cards, that sort of thing."

"Of course, Mr. Spector." He buzzed his intercom and asked for a file to be brought in.

"Nothing the matter, is there? Miss Olive was particularly eager to make sure everything went as you asked her. She wrote me out instructions."

Spector was out of voice. He shook his head. His lips pressed together and they forced his face into an unwitting smile.

A girl arrived with the files. She had a beauty mark too. Perhaps it was the same girl. Spector couldn't remember.

There were only a few papers to look at. On top was a cover memo from Cynthia. He recognized her elegant slant, loops reaching in parallels. The first time he had seen it she was opening a dossier for Edgar Parish, considering his loan. You could see in that writing the little girl bent over her Palmer Method workbook, the sister at her shoulder, angling the paper so the letters reached out like sloops heeling in the wind.

The memo was matter-of-fact. A Mr. Spector had been in on Saturday the 11th. He was a longtime resident of Manhattan. Used to be in finance. She had opened his account. He intended to deposit a seven-figure sum. He wanted an interest account or a short-term CD, because he would probably be removing the funds shortly. There would be two signatures on the account. Mr. Spector hadn't given the name of the second person but would send in cards.

There was an authorization slip opening the account. Spector had signed it. Someone—it must have been Cynthia—had typed in his address, Social Security number, and the names of the authorized signatories. Both of them. A signature card. Spector had signed that as well. A second signature was below his. A deposit slip showed the transfer from the Panamanian bank. And a withdrawal slip, a week later, back to Panama. Same amount, different account number. The second authorized name had signed the withdrawal slip. The slant had been arighted, but the hand was recognizable. And Spector had to smile at the cryptonym. Lila Parish.

33

Lauren accepted the news more easily than Spector expected. More easily than Spector had.

"Gone? You had it and it's gone?"

"I had it and it's gone."

"And you can't get it back? I mean, a million bucks, man. It's not as if it's a stray cat."

He had taken Lauren from his desk and they were walking down Sixth. They passed Radio City, where lines of people were filing off the morning's first Grey Line bus.

"What can I tell you? It's gone."

"What makes me suspect you didn't have too firm a grip on it?"

"Yeah. You could say that."

Lauren nodded slowly.

"So what do we do? Hard to buy this company with nothing."

"Very hard."

His partner breathed an audible sigh.

"Not sure I was intended to be an entrepreneur. That was too good to be true. I'm back to tote that barge."

Spector nodded in response. They stood on the corner of Forty-ninth. Spector had nothing more to say.

"We gonna play any more tennis before the spring?"

"Doubt it. I think my fancy club will be the first casualty of the new economic regime."

" 'Fraid of that. Not surprised. You gonna get your exercise just like us common folk now. Fighting for crusts of bread in the street."

"Lift that bale," Spector said. "But in the spring . . ." It came out a half-question.

"Shit, yes. Soon as it warms up, we'll go at it again. I mean, how many ex-millionaires do I know that I can beat?"

He couldn't recall why he had agreed to see the man. The telephone plaint had been carping, obsequious. Spector must forgive him for checking up like this, but he was really eager to talk. To discuss Cynthia Olive. He could assure Mr. Spector he wasn't going to pry into his personal life.

Now he remembered. Who else could he talk to about her? It was better than nothing.

When he opened the apartment door, he saw a pinch-faced man with horn-rimmed glasses. He invited him in.

"We can sit there," he said, "or in the kitchen if you'd like a table to write on."

"This will be fine."

The visitor took the armchair, and Spector sat in the one from the dinette set. He hadn't moved it back since coming home.

Record jackets were strewn around the floor like throw pillows. Spector turned down the music.

"You like Monk?" he asked absently.

"I beg your pardon?" said the man.

"Never mind. I'm sorry, tell me your name again."

The man handed him a card. "Gellhorn. Philip Gellhorn. It's right there." Spector looked at the card and tossed it on the coffee table.

"We picked up your name from the bank where she worked. You did go on a date with her a week or so ago?"

"Yes, I did. Not exactly a date."

"Central Park Zoo, wasn't it? Very romantic. We've been watching her, Mr. Spector. You just happened by. And then she disappears. I've made this my personal case. And I'm chief investigator for the company."

Spector waited. He thought Gellhorn wanted to be congratulated on his promotion. That's not why I'm here, he thought. Tell me something about her.

"We're just wondering if you knew her well. If you have any ideas about where she might have gone."

"No, I really don't, Mr. Gellhorn. I haven't seen or heard from her since. I didn't even know where she lived."

"We know that, Mr. Spector. I've figured that much out. You must have met her that day at the bank, dated her once. Platonic relationship. Didn't go home with her." He pushed his glasses back onto the bridge of his nose and stretched wide his eyes in pleasure.

"Am I correct?"

"Correct."

"We're nothing if not thorough. And we know about you, your exceptional career in investment banking. It was pure chance that you and she should cross paths. We figure she had a confederate, and that she's gone to meet him. Believe me, she is not your type. She's one tough little enchilada."

They chatted for a few more moments. How easy it would be to disappear in this city. Spector said he had never thought of that. Oh, yes, said Gellhorn. Right here. Especially if you're Puerto Rican. Spector promised to let him know if he heard from Cynthia again.

"But I have to tell you, I doubt that I will. We didn't really hit it off."

Spector again sat facing the window. He realized it wasn't coincidence. Shelley always let him enter first and Spector always chose to sit with his back toward the room, so he could look outside. What was there to see?

"I can't eat the pickles any more."

Spector had no reply. The remark didn't call for one.

"My digestion's not been so hot lately. My doc wants me to take it easy. Used to be I could eat cement."

Shelley helped himself to a green tomato from the bottle of brine on the table. Their waiter came by, balancing two baskets of rolls on two bowls of soup.

"You put our order in?" Shelley asked him.

"No. I sent it to Gorbachev. He'll know what to do with it."

"Now I understand," Shelley answered. "That's why it takes so long to get a sandwich. It's coming from Moscow." The waiter kept going. "By way of Pinsk," Shelley called to his back.

"Now I understand," he repeated to Spector.

"Shelley, relax. We're in no rush."

"You're in no rush. You're retired. Me, I got a contractor, he'll use my veins for pipes if I don't get back there and take care of him." The tomato was the size of a baseball. Shelley sliced it into sections and put the largest in his mouth.

It was another cold day. Outside, steam rose from the manhole covers like sails.

"So that's all? No other news?"

"Nothing of interest."

"Who said interest? You diddle around in England, play a little tennis, make a run at an insurance company, and can't come up with the money. That's it for four months?"

"That's it."

The waiter came with their order. "Corned beef on onion. Tea." He named the dishes as if his patrons might not recognize them. "Seltzer, tongue on rye." He looked at Spector, deadpan, and tilted his head toward Shelley. "He needs tongue. He doesn't have enough of his own."

"This used to be a restaurant," Shelley said in mock confidence, for the waiter to hear. "Now it's a comedy shop." He spread the top piece of his bread with mustard, placed it carefully back on the sandwich, and took a bite.

They ate in silence. When Shelley spoke again, it was on a new subject.

"You know, Joanie and you should never have split. You should have tried to make a go of it." He swallowed. "I never say this to her, you understand. But I really think you were good for each other. In my view, you have a lot in common."

"You think so?"

"Absolutely." Shelley took time to chew. "You're both brainy, ambitious. Good kids. You both have your head up your ass." He pointed with his sandwich. "You go away to find yourself, you can't. She's going out with a nice man, a dentist from South Orange, she tells me he's too nice. Two peas in a pod."

Spector fished out his tea bag from the pot with a spoon, wrapped the string around it, and squeezed out the water. He laughed. There was something to what Shelley said.

"So. What's next? What are you going to do?"

"I don't know. My old firm called me. M-and-A work is really heating up, and all they have in the department are a bunch of adolescents. Imagine, I'm thirty-one and they're luring me back for my silver hair."

"Interested?"

"I don't think so. Might be. You gave me a good idea last time. I thought I'd see if you had any more."

"I did?"

"You told me to try robbing banks."

"Right." Shelley laughed. "Good idea. Low cost of goods sold. Of course, you won't be able to deduct this lunch."

It was great corned beef. It was the best sandwich Spector had had in months.

"Joanie asks about you." Shelley sounded hesitant, uncommonly so. "She knows we keep in touch."

Spector nodded. "Say hi for me."

"That's it? Hi?"

"That's it."

"Let me write it down. I want to get it right." Shelley reached into the jar for a pickle.

"I'll tell you something. Sandwiches are okay here, but the pickles keep them in business."

Spector watched him eat it.

"Says she wrote you a note, never heard."

"She wanted some files. I sent them to her. On a metals account. We lost our shirt."

"You got a shirt on. You must have had two. You send her the files, fine. No note? No 'Enclosed please find the files'? This is your ex-wife."

"Shelley, if you're trying to make your heartburn contagious, you're succeeding. Tell her hi and I hope she's getting along."

"Better." He paused. "She brings over breakfast, you know. Every Sunday. With the paper. One day I could tell her, Bring a little extra."

Spector laughed.

"What do you think? I don't want to push, but you could do worse. Coffee, a little grapefruit."

"Sure. That might be nice."

"You want some pie? I may have a piece of pie. I lost two pounds last week."

"You look it. You look great."

Shelley was pleased. He wiped his mouth with a napkin and pushed himself an inch back from the table.

"You know what you need?"

"No." Spector gave a quiet laugh. "What do I need?"

Shelley raised his hand and twisted in his chair to signal their waiter. Then he turned back to face Spector, but he kept his arm on high, waving.

"A new life. New place, new name, new occupation. Just pack up and reappear somewhere."

The waiter was standing at the front watching the passing crowd on Broadway. Spector could see the man's eyes in the reflection of the large plate-glass window. He was aware of Shelley's flagging hand, and he wore a thin smile.

"You know, Shelley, I think you're on to something. I think you may be absolutely right."

385120

DUC

Ducker, Bruce.

Bankroll

900316

$16.95

DATE		
MAR - 2 1990		
MAR 16 1990		
1 5 NOV 1995		
0 9 JUL 1998		